Starlight and Stilettos

Katlyn Rose

Published by Katie Rose, 2023.

This is a work of fiction. Similarities to real people, places, or events are entirely coincidental.

STARLIGHT AND STILETTOS

First edition. September 12, 2023.

Copyright © 2023 Katlyn Rose.

ISBN: 979-8223325437

Written by Katlyn Rose.

To the many women who helped shape my life in my younger years and to the women who standing beside me today. Mom, you were a force to be reckoned with even as quiet as you were, thank you.

"Beneath the city lights and shadows of the past, we dance between who we were and who we dare to become, finding freedom in the starlight and strength in the stilettos that carry us forward."

Katlyn Rose

Imagine a place where the fabric of time folds in on itself, where the past, present, and future coexist in a delicate, shimmering balance. In this place, you might find yourself walking down a quiet path, and as you turn a corner, you come face-to-face with *you*. Not the you of today, but the you of a different time, a version of yourself you once were, or perhaps one you've yet to become.

The first self you meet is your child self. Their eyes are wide with wonder, unburdened by the weight of years. They carry a boundless curiosity, a spark of imagination that has yet to be dimmed by doubt or fear. They tug at your hand, eager to show you the world through their eyes, where every shadow hides a secret and every corner turns into an adventure. In their presence, you remember what it feels like to dream without limits, to believe in the impossible. You smile, wondering how you ever let go of that fearless wonder.

Further along the path, you encounter your adolescent self. Awkward and uncertain, they wear their insecurities like a second skin. Yet, beneath the surface, there's a fierce determination, a longing to be seen, understood, and loved. They speak of dreams that once seemed so vital, of heartbreaks that felt like the end of the world. You listen, feeling a pang of tenderness for this version of you who stumbled through the tumult of growing up. You want to tell them that it gets better, that the struggles they endure will shape them into someone strong, resilient, and wise.

And then, there's your young adult self, bold, ambitious, and hungry for life. They are filled with the energy of someone who believes time is infinite, that the world is theirs for the taking. They speak of plans, of love, of nights spent chasing stars and mornings filled with quiet hope. Their optimism is contagious, and you feel a spark reignite within you. But you also see the cracks forming, the pressures of expectation, the beginnings of compromises made for survival. You want to tell them to hold on to their fire, to be gentler with themselves, but you know they must learn this on their own.

As you walk further, you meet your present self, the you of today. This self stands taller, their shoulders set with the weight of lived experience. They carry scars, some visible, others hidden deep within. Yet, their eyes are steady, their voice calm. They've weathered storms, faced fears, and made peace with uncertainties. You feel a deep sense of recognition and gratitude for this version of yourself who continues to navigate life's complexities with courage and grace.

And finally, you come upon your future self. They stand at the edge of the path, shrouded in a soft, golden light. They do not speak, but their presence is comforting, reassuring. Their eyes are filled with a quiet wisdom, a knowing that comes from a life well-lived. In their gaze, you see peace, fulfillment, and a profound acceptance of all that has been and all that is to come. You feel a surge of hope, knowing that no matter where your journey leads, you will arrive whole, complete.

In this timeless place, you realize that every version of yourself, past, present, and future, is a thread in the tapestry of your existence. Each self carries its own lessons, joys, and sorrows, contributing to the person you are continually becoming. You are a mosaic of experiences, a symphony of moments, and every self you meet is a vital part of the beautiful, complex story that is *you*.

CHAPTER 1

Cassie stormed out of the observatory like a bull charging the gate. The anger emanating from her cleared a path all the way to her car. Not even her friends tried to stand in her way. Once behind the wheel, the tears flowed. Hot, angry tears that matched her mood. Cassie leaned forward, placing her arms across the steering wheel and rested her head on her arms. She let the tears flow freely.

That backstabber, Tyler, had ruined any chance of her presenting her research to the board to be able to delve deeper into the discovery she had made. The college had helped her wrangle the opportunity to use the observatory in Tennessee, and now that was gone as well. It wasn't as grand as some, and basically used to teach, but she had been granted free time if she would help with some of the classes that came through. Cassie gladly accepted.

In order to study her stars and set about sharing an idea that there are multiple parallel universes, "The universe being so big, what are the possibilities," she had to reach deep into the skies and see if the answers were there. The university gave her four weeks in Tennessee to find her proof. Cassie wiped her face as she sat up, putting her best face forward and made a beeline for the exit, never looking back. Okay, a quick glance. She was afraid the tears would start again.

Smiling, she stopped at the guard gate and turned in her pass, keys, and embossed key card with all the computer codes, and said goodbye to the guards. She felt the sting of tears again. This time, as she drove away, she didn't look back.

Until three weeks ago, Cassie spent all her time studying the universe and teaching theory to college students. Since receiving her PhD in her early 20s, her goal was to somehow, miraculously prove her parallel universe theory. She had discovered stars, seen black holes, talked with astronauts, and done just about everything an astronomer could do, except have use of an observatory telescope for any length of time. Then somehow, Tyler had found out about her other job, made a big deal out of it, which caused the university to shun her and take away her funding.

"Well," she exclaimed out loud, "I'll just show those busy bodies that I mean business about my universe. They won't have a choice but to believe me."

Cassie drove to her hotel in Brentwood, packed her bags, equipment, and notes, paid her bill, and headed out of Tennessee, back to Dallas and home. She had come to love this area, but Texas had what she needed. She had business to take care of and it would be best done face to face. She really hoped this wasn't some good old boy thing, and she wanted explanations for cutting her off on the accusations from one idiot without contacting her first.

Cassie called her best friend, Drake, two days later to let him know she was back and would be in that Friday. Drake was Cassie's business manager and ran things if she had to travel. They met in college and had been friends for 27 years. There were no secrets. Drake told her to take her time, all was well, even take another day if needed. "Nope." Cassie thought, she needed to burn some energy.

Cassie spent the afternoon unpacking, made a quick trip to the university to pack what few personal belongings were there, and returned to her townhouse. No more teaching to fill her days, which brought another threat of tears. She would find a way to finish her research. She knew people. She could go to Denton when needed. Not ideal, but the telescope was better than hers.

The next couple of days, Cassie put her work notes in order and worked on a short proposal for what she thought she might have found while in Tennessee. Spotted only once, she wasn't sure if the anomaly was there or not but would have to wait for a miracle to be able to find out. Her telescope just didn't have the power, and a rooftop in Dallas wasn't ideal for trying to find the area she had noted. She hoped that one of the observatories close by would yield what she had found in the stars.

Checking the time that Friday, Cassie saw she had a couple more hours before her other work so she skimmed through emails she had ignored for the last couple of days, deleting most, flagging those she would respond to later. Glancing at the clock, it was time to leave.

Cassie was not the run of the mill type of professor of astrology. She had inherited an almost defunct business from the aunt who raised her until she turned 16, when her aunt died, leaving her a townhouse near the business, a country home outside of Dallas, and a very large cash inheritance to go with it. After paying her remaining tuition, she sunk most of the balance into restoring and reviving GalUp, never realizing how big a hit it would be.

Besides her PhD in astrology, Cassie had minored in business, theater, and dance choreography. The latter mostly for exercise, but then found it a welcome break from teaching and staring at stars all day. Drake, being a business major, scoffed at first, but then joined her in dance and found he was quite good at it. When she told him about GalUp, he again scoffed, but helped her with the finances and the staff.

Several years after that, she bought the building beside her, remodeled, and made the corner block a two-story theater and restaurant, Texas style. Drake questioned her every move but backed her up. GalUp was a hit, both in the theater and the restaurant. She was the main attraction.

The once rundown area housed many well-built buildings that had been allowed to fall into various states of disrepair. Auntie Nev had managed to keep GalUp fairly updated and clean, but around it everything was empty. When Cassie inherited the building and saw the potential opportunity with the other buildings, she put a plan in place to create an upscale entertainment block, and purchased when she could afford to, leasing it for some type of club, restaurant, and eventually allowed clothing stores in. Most levels were rehabilitated to high-end apartments and office space. She did very well with this venture and enjoyed the idea of seeing life restored in that part of the city.

GalUp was the main attraction. She had a marquee that resembled the ones from the 30s and 40s and highlighted different acts daily. The front entrance was built movie theater style, with the hostess in a small glass enclosed booth, greeting customers and calling into the second hostess, who seated each customer.

Upon entering GalUp, people were greeted with a posh seating area and small bar if there was a wait, being able to view the show while enjoying light appetizers and drinks. The second level was the main dining area for those interested in dinner and a show. Built balcony style with the back level being on risers so the customer was able to see without straining.

Cassie entered GalUp from the employee's entrance tonight, not yet ready for anyone to see her. Quickly sneaking into hers and Drake's office, she walked to the large view mirror and scanned the growing crowd. It looked like high-roller night tonight and was already quite packed. Spotting Drake, Cassie texted him to let him know she was there, watching as he kindly disengaged from the woman next to him, and smiling slightly at her crest-fallen face.

Drake himself, at 47, was stunning to look at. Cassie admitted to herself that if they weren't best friends, she might try to capture him herself, but knew he was a confirmed bachelor. Where she was soft colored, Drake was dark. Thick, dark hair so black it had a blue hue to it at times. Dark skin that glowed gold. Lips that were full but not ridiculously so and thinned incredibly when ticked or perturbed. But what caught everyone's attention who knew or met him was his shocking blue eyes, not light but deep dark blue. People swore he could see right into their souls.

Cassie smiled while watching him swim through the crowd, speaking to people as he headed up, finally getting through. She went to the credenza, poured them both a drink and waited. As debonaire as he looked on the floor, that's how flustered he looked coming through the door. He looked upset and peeved but flashed his award-winning smile and gave Cassie a huge hug. She giggled softly as he put her down.

"Don't ever be gone that long again:" he scolded. "It has been pure D hell here." His accent gave his Texas roots away. Deep and rumbling but definitely Texan.

"Hello to you too." Cassie giggled. "Seems you're the hit of the floor tonight."

Drake glared at her and plopped on the oversized sofa, patting the space beside him. Cassie plopped beside him and leaned into his arm. She felt so comfortable and secure when they sat like this.

After a few quiet and comfortable minutes, Drake spoke. "So, what made our galloping astronomer come back early?"

Cassie heaved a huge sigh, stood up, and told him everything, finishing with, "And it's not like I had done a single thing wrong. They seemed to think my life should revolve only around stars, and not the people kind. That a-hole, Tyler, made this place sound trashy to them."

"Oh babe, that little twit isn't worth all the anger bottled up in there." Drake soothed, tapping her on the temple.

"I've worked my tail off for the university. Bounced through their hoops, did all the good girl things so I can work on my theory. I guess I'm just disappointed they chose him over me. He's not even finished with his dissertation. Which, by the way, is totally moronic."

"Do tell." Drake said. And Cassie did.

Using air quotes, "Why There Can't Be Other Life in the Universe." Cassie spat out. "I mean, really!? In this day and age? He's literally using just the Bible to write it. Even that book hints at other forms of life. I think his daddy, wait, momma has too much money influence is the problem."

"Well, we've heard for years that she's the preferred flavor with all the alumni." He sniggered rudely.

"Damn Drake, call 'em like you see 'em much?"

"Babe, let's talk later. You're here, we've got a full house, go mingle. Take some aggression out on those hot, rich, young studs down there." Drake said, pointing to a corner of young men.

"I may need anger therapy, but just no. Unless you put a Tyler face on them and let me use them for target practice."

"Hon," Drake stood behind her, "Don't chew them up just yet. One of our wealthy patrons set this up for them. Skin without the trash. Guess I'd better recommend you dancing instead. Actually, you being here couldn't be better timing. We need this to be a superstar night."

"Dang Drake," she butted against his chest, "So you're now leading the cow to slaughter. I'm scared of you. Go tell Thomas to get ready." Handing him a CD. "New routine. Meant to kick butt and burn energy."

"Where does it come from, my dear?"

"It's my alter ego. She slips in from the unknown." Cassie smiled as Drake left. She went to her dressing room to prepare.

CHAPTER 2

Sitting at her dressing table in GalUp, Cassie knew she looked good tonight. At 45, she was still svelte and elegant. Piercing green eyes, surrounded by naturally dark and long lashes, which were enhanced with stage makeup to make them greener and darker. Her slightly pouty lips were coated with a glossy dusty rose lipstick that gave her complexion the soft hue of a golden tan that was in reality her natural color. She chose to keep her golden-brown hair long and softly feathered when down but no strays when pulled up. This facial ensemble drew the attention of men, both wanted and unwanted, and occasionally a woman or two.

Cassie stood in front of the mirror, checking for any flaws. As she examined herself, she thought, "This really is my alter ego. Dark and almost cynical looking."

She had enhanced her hair to make it darker and with the makeup, looked sultry and seductive. Her special bustier kept her ample girls locked in tight, and she would definitely need that for tonight. As she snapped her stilettos in place, her phone rang. Who would be calling at this hour on her personal cell?

"Hey babe." It was Drake.

"What the heck, Drake. I'm meditating." She growled.

"Well, meditate this." He growled back. "We have some very special guests tonight. They've been here for the past three nights in hopes of catching a glimpse of Landy Cassandra."

"Who the hell is it, Drake?" Cassie exclaimed. "No one knows I'm back."

"It seems these people do. In fact, their comment, 'We heard' was mentioned." Drake seemed pensive and almost cheerful at the same time.

"Well, seat them somewhere nice and comp their first drink. I'm not coming out until I'm done." Cassie spit out.

"Don't you want to know who they are?" Drake drawled the question out.

All of the sudden Cassie got cold feet and started shaking. She knew better than to ask but did anyway.

"Are they a group of nerdy people who look like they've been sucking pickles?"

"You hit the nail on the head! Score one for the science nerd."

Cassie swallowed hard. "Give them the best seat in the house if you can. Tell Thomas I'll ring when ready." She hung up with shaking hands, feeling like this was her first audition. And well, in a way it was. These people had known nothing of her life outside of the university until a few days ago.

She sat down at her makeup table and stared hard at the mirror. "My alter ego." She said out loud. "An alter universe. What would my alter-self be doing right now?"

As Cassie stared, she felt the world around her darken. She swore she felt a shift and things around her change. Staring back at her was, her, but slightly different. It looked like a younger, softer, but edgy her. The figure in the mirror smiled slightly and Cassie heard her speak. Or thought she did.

The voice was hers, younger sounding, "You've got this gal. Show 'em what you're really made of." And then she was herself again.

"What the hell was that!?" Cassie said to herself. "I must be going crazy now. Crap."

Cassie only required three songs per set from each of her dancers. One sultry, one edgy fun, and one risqué or sung, but not raunchy as all dancers filled the stages on the third song. For the dancers with a mediocre voice, she allowed lip syncing, but it had to be perfect. To this day, she had only one person fail her in that. Tonight, she would show them her dancer side.

Cassie watched as Drake seated her ex, pain in the butt co-worker and others from the university. Her stomach knotted and she felt very tense, but almost as quick, a sense of peace surrounded her. She knew exactly how the evening was going to turn out but threw out a quick prayer just in case.

Cassie's mind carried her back to that horrid day a few days ago, remembering the teleconference with the very people sitting front center stage.

"Dr. Hunter, it seems we found out that you have an unsavory night life."

"Excuse me?"

The head of her department snorted. "We found through an external source, that you are a stripper. What do you have to say about that?"

Cassie was shocked. Who could have found out about her business? It was not a strip club. She was livid. "I did not realize my activities after work were being monitored."

"Are you saying you are a stripper?"

"I am not saying anything. My time away from the university is just that, my time." She replied coldly.

"But you're not denying it."

"Nothing I do on my off time affects the university. I make sure of that."

"Then you do strip when you're not teaching?" He seemed determined to get that answer from her. Cassie was equally determined not to answer it at all.

"Who gave you this information? I would like to meet them face-to-face. I will not be accused of something I am not doing." She literally growled.

"You are not answering the question, Dr. Hunter. This implies a lot to me. It does not matter who the source is or where the information came from," he sternly told her, "your extracurricular activities can cause harm to the university's reputation."

"My extracurricular activities, as you call them, have never had any effect on my job or the university. I spend more time here doing my job than there doing a different job." Cassie became more upset as the conversation progressed.

"Dr. Hunter, either confirm or deny. We have the right to know if what you are doing will cause issues here. You are sounding very defensive, and, in my mind, that means you are hiding something. Are you going to confirm or deny that you have an unsavory night life?"

Cassie happened to glance up at that moment and saw Tyler standing in the doorway smirking. It then dawned on her that he probably had been listening in on her conversations with Drake and relayed incorrect information to her superiors. Incorrect information that could cost her the grant she and worked so hard to be gifted.

With a sigh, Cassie realized they knew she danced, thought she was a stripper, but didn't know she owned GalUp. "Well, since Tyler gave you his skewed version, I'll give you the truth." Cassie looked pointedly at Tyler. "Tyler, you might as well join us, so you have your facts right."

Tyler at least had the grace to blush as he moved into the small office and sat down.

"First, what I am going to do is expand the video conference call so you can see me and Tyler, hopefully judge on my reaction, and not rely on the opinion of a backstabber, as to whether or not I'm lying." Cassie tapped a couple of buttons, and the screen showed there to be five of the governing board there.

"I am not, nor have I ever been a stripper. I find that profession revolting and demeaning. And while I understand that is the only job some ladies can get, I have not had that misfortune. I am a choreographer and dancer. However, my love of astrology and the stars is far greater than my love of dance, which is why I teach and research. I am a burlesque dancer, which means I do not strip."

One of the other prefects chimed in. "You mean there's a difference? I've seen burlesque, you're still practically naked."

"Classily undressed, would be a better description." Cassie answered. "Where I work is very classy and tasteful and they don't like being stereotyped like that. Very unlike many of the burlesque houses today. We pride ourselves on that. There is also a dinner theater should one choose dinner and a show."

"But you still dance half naked" another prefect asked.

Tyler chose that moment to add his two cents. "I heard her on the phone talking about strippers and how she could out dance any stripper around."

Cassie thought a moment, trying to remember that conversation. Shit. She remembered. "It seems that Tyler only heard part of that conversation. My manager told me that a troupe of professional strippers were trying to get the company to let them perform. When they were turned down, they filed a discrimination suit. I told him somewhere in that conversation, I could out dance any stripper anywhere, fully clothed, and if they didn't like being turned down, we could have a dance challenge anywhere but GalUp. That is what that little twit heard, but only chose to tell one part of the story." Cassie glared at Tyler.

The only female prefect looked disgusted as she spoke. "Stripper or not, it is an improper vocation for a teaching member of our staff to have. What if one of your students or our alumni were to see you? How would we explain your state of public indecency to them?"

That comment blew Cassie's mind. "Excuse me? Do you see what the majority of the students are wearing? Hell, even dressed out at GalUp, I have less showing."

"Hold there for a moment. You have at least confirmed you do dance." The head prefect spoke. "We'll be right with you." He muted the sound, and Cassie saw them moving out of the camera's view.

Cassie glared at Tyler. Since becoming her assistant at the observatory, she realized all the trouble she had and was having came from him. She just thought it was because she was cramming years of hypothesis into four short weeks. Tyler had questioned everything she wanted to do and was trying to do to the point of being obnoxiously intrusive. "Crap. And screwed me over." She thought.

A polite cough brought her attention back to the screen. "Dr. Hunter, we have come to the conclusion that, even if you don't strip, that type of dancing, should you be found out, would be detrimental to the university."

A different prefect spoke. "If one of your students or a member of our staff were to see you in that environment, it would as if we condoned that type of behavior."

And again, the head prefect spoke. "It is our decision to withdraw funding on your research and suspend you teaching until this matter is settled."

Cassie gasped.

"This withdrawal is contingent on your decision today. Should you give up your extracurricular activities and change your area of research, the funding continues."

"Give up my research?" Cassie cried out.

"The things you are looking for do not exist. Your research seems more of an obsession. Find a new constellation or something other than parallel universe. That is old hat anyway."

That confirmed again to Cassie that Tyler had given over everything she had discussed with him, but in his own skewed version. This wasn't and either or, this was a getting even.

"I'll tell you what." She spat out. "I've done what my tenure required and more. Nothing has ever been done to hurt the reputation of the university or my department. If you choose to believe the idiot version of some dimwitted undergrad, trying to get his nonsensical PhD, fine. I will not be threatened for what I do when I am not here. Especially as it has caused no harm to anyone. And trust me when I say this, it's not over." She disconnected the conference, tears streaming down her cheeks and yelled at Tyler to get out.

As Cassie entered the observatory, she sensed someone or something but didn't see anything. She neatly and calmly filed all her research notes, gathered her personal equipment, and placed it all near the door. She went to her office and packed her personal belongings, then pulled her car as close to the door as possible.

Returning to gather her things, she saw Tyler rifling through her boxes. "What the hell, Tyler!"

"I am taking possession of your original notes regarding your project and returning them to the university."

"Like hell!" She leaned into his space. "Either remove your hands from my belongings or I will remove them for you."

"But the prefect said to..." Quickly moving away as Cassie raised a fist.

"You can tell the prefects where they can go. This is my work and only the good Lord above can take them away. Touch anything else and I will break your fingers." She bowed up to Tyler at that point. "You know what? Get out of my space, out of here until I am done."

When Tyler stalled, Cassie, who never used force, grabbed the sleeve of his lab coat, and dragged him out, locking the door behind him. After loading her car, she unlocked the door and hunted Tyler down.

"You are a sorry piece of crap." She yelled at him. "Never once did I think you would stoop so low as you did. Have a good time trying to disprove my theory. And by the way, don't think I'm stupid enough to not know you copied my notes off the computer. You won't find a thing but useless drivel."

She stormed out of the office to her car.

CHAPTER 3

As Cassie came out of that memory, she noted one thing. Something or someone was with her that day, keeping her relatively calm, cool, and collected. She would have to reflect on that later. She had to get in tune with herself as there were two songs before her time on the main stage.

Her phone rang, startling her. "Hello?"

It was Drake. "You don't have to do this, Cass." He sounded concerned. "Let the lawyers handle it."

"No Drake." Cassie breathed out. "They must see they were wrong and misled by that dipshit. The attorneys will have their day, tonight is mine."

"All right, sweetie. Thomas knows to pull out all the stops tonight."

Cassie kissed at Drake and went into meditation mode as she made her way to the platform under center stage. No one spoke to her. They could see she was oblivious to the world around her. Everyone backstage moved to the main floor. They felt something extraordinary was about to happen. The whole of backstage was empty, except for the sound and effects crew. They could see everything from their stations as well as their monitors. Cassie never heard Thomas introduce her.

"Ladies and gentlemen, after an absence of a few weeks, it is with immense pleasure that GalUp presents to you, a lady that outshines the stars. Her brightness overwhelms the night sky with a never-ending glow. A voice who stops the angels above in their tracks. I present to you, the one, the only, Lady Cassandra."

The green 'go' light flashed and the stage above opened, lifting Cassie slowly upwards. As thick smoke rolled across the stage, enveloping Cassie, it gave her a ghostly appearance. As everything was locked in place and the music started, not a sound could be heard throughout the whole building. The place wasn't even this quiet when it was closed. Anticipation hung heavy as every single person held their breath.

Lady Cassandra stood dead center middle stage with her hands raised above her and her head thrown back. The soft gray green scarves fluttered gently as the breeze from the stage drifted across. The music began to rise. Cassie felt as if "something" had again taken her over as she began to flow into the music. She felt almost as if she floated out of herself and was watching the show instead of being the show.

As the first hard beat hit, Cassie began the dance of a thousand seductresses. Her eyes made contact with those closest to her, promising imaginative, exotic things, forever locking them to her. Her body undulated erotically to the strong beat, hypnotizing both men and women alike who watched the seductive moves of her body, causing flush after flush to move through the crowd.

They watched her slink and shimmy, losing the scarves one by one, revealing a soft-hued body in a short, tennis type skirt and a shimmering top with billowing sleeves. Cassie felt herself flowing, gently releasing all the pent-up anger, feeling unbelievably sexy and goddess like.

As the last scarf released from her body, the beat of the music hardened and became tough and strong. Thomas had not paused to give her a breather, somehow knowing she didn't need one.

The beat picked up and Cassie felt herself grow strong and wild. She felt anger possess her and she popped, twisted, kicked, and sailed as the music grew faster and chaotic. Never missing a beat, she danced the dance of a woman finding herself, her inner most, wild woman. When the music abruptly stopped, she drew herself from the floor and stepped up to the mic that had mysteriously appeared.

You wear the weight of a thousand nights,
Shadows clinging to your frame.
You've danced with doubt under dim streetlights,
Hiding tears from the world in shame.
You've fought battles no one could see,
Bruised and broken, yet you stood free.
This song is for you, my sister, my friend,
For the storm inside you that'll never bend.
Oh, hear me now, all you fierce, wild hearts,
From the ashes, you rise, playing your part.
With every scar, you wear your crown,
No one can keep this fire down.
Through fears and tears, you stand and fight,
You are the dawn breaking through the night.
There were nights you screamed into the void,
Hoping someone would hear your name.
You stitched your wounds with threads of courage,
And stood tall through the deepest pain.
You've been silenced, chained, and cast aside,
Yet within you, the universe resides.
You've felt the weight of dreams denied,
But your spirit soared, undignified.
Oh, hear me now, all you fierce, wild hearts,
From the ashes, you rise, playing your part.
With every scar, you wear your crown,
No one can keep this fire down.
Through fears and tears, you stand and fight,
You are the dawn breaking through the night.
To the mothers, the daughters, the warriors unseen,

You carry the strength of all who've been.
Your voice is thunder, your soul's a flame,
And no one can ever dim your name.
You are more than your trials, more than your pain,
You're the sunlight after the rain.
Oh, hear me now, all you fierce, wild hearts,
Through the struggle, you've become the art.
With every scar, you wear your crown,
You rise, you reign, you'll never back down.
Through fears and tears, you claim your light,
You are the stars, you are the night.
So rest now, my sister, let your soul take flight,
You've conquered the darkness, you've won the fight.
In your eyes, the cosmos, in your heart, the sea,
You're everything you were meant to be.
From fear to love, from tear to smile,
You've walked every road, every mile.
This song is yours, for you've come so far,
You are my sister, my guiding star.

Cassie sang to all the women everywhere. She sang of the fears, the tears, the struggles, and of the triumph of being. Her song called to hearts and souls alike. As the song neared its end, her sultry, smokey voice resonated with peace and love. The moment of silence after Cassie finished was instantly filled with thunderous applause, so loud that it could be heard outside the building, making people wonder what happened.

As for Cassie, she looked at the stunned crowd with the same expression she was seeing on their faces, wondering what she had just done because she remembered nothing of it. Bowing to the crowd, she walked off stage to the waiting Drake. The look in his eyes told her everything she needed to know. Whatever she had done out there made an impression and would be talked about for days to come.

"Babe," Drake spoke huskily, "I don't know what just took place, but you damn near set GalUp on fire."

Cassie laughed shakily. "Honestly Drake, I don't know either. It's like something possessed me and took over. I should be totally exhausted and yet I'm not."

Cassie then noticed, for the first time in a long time, how gorgeous Drake really was. The smoldering look in his eyes caused an all-encompassing heat to run through her body. She felt herself flush under his gaze. Turning away, she placed her hands on her cheeks.

The main floor guard interrupted them. "Cass, people at the main table are asking for you."

Cassie turned to him. "Tell them it will be 20 minutes."

As she walked through the main dressing area, she was congratulated by dancers, singers, wait staff, and stagehands. She thanked them as she walked on, telling everyone how proud she was of them. In many, she saw tears, but not of sadness, of joy and understanding. Cassie felt lighter and freer than she had in years.

Drake poured Cassie a drink and shooed her to the bathroom. The desire in his eyes made her shiver with a deep desire of her own. She knew he would come to her if she asked but she didn't. They had agreed years before to not start a relationship. Work and play were not allowed.

Cassie heard Drake leave and turned to the mirror in her private dressing room. Looking back was the same Cassie as earlier. Her but not her. She stood silently and studied the face. It seemed slightly thinner and younger, but the same. The eyes were sparkling, and a look of contented joy filled them.

Cassie smiled, the image smiled too. And then Cassie heard the words, "Well done, girl. Well done." As quickly as the image appeared it was gone, but the total sense of accomplishment remained.

Cassie knew beyond a shadow of a doubt that her next life had begun. She knew she would probably no longer be a professor and knew equally well that her needed answers from the stars would always be waiting when she went looking. For now, she would deal with the pickle-faced people from the university and life would go on from there.

Changing into a sexy, form fitting evening dress that complimented her from head to toe, touching up her makeup and hair, Cassie made her way downstairs to the "pickle" table where her colleagues were waiting.

"Ladies, gentlemen." Cassie nodded, looking down on them. "Definitely pickle faces." She thought to herself, then aloud. "I hope dinner was to your liking."

They all nodded affirmatively as the head prefect invited her to join them, which she did, baring her legs to high thigh for all to see. Several interruptions later, the conversation she had been waiting for finally began. The music being so loud, Cassie recommended moving to a back booth to better understand each other.

The older female prefect spoke first. "That was a very intriguing performance, Dr. Hunter. I assume that was done for our benefit?"

"You assume incorrectly." Cassie responded, causing the woman to blush. "That performance was for my audience. They at least appreciate the fact that I don't strip, and I give them their money's worth."

The woman cleared her throat. "My apologies. None of the other acts seem to be as charismatic as yours."

"None of the other acts are me."

"I see. Very impressive. If you threw yourself into your university work as hard, there's no telling what you could accomplish." The woman stated sarcastically.

Cassie hackles immediately rose, and she felt a hot flush hit her stomach. Clenching her hands in her lap, she silently counted to ten, then, never breaking eye contact, spoke directly to the woman.

"This will be the last time I speak to you, any of you, without my attorney present."

The head prefect held a hand up to Cassie. "Dr. Hunter, we are not here to bully or threaten."

"You just did."

"Dr. Hunter," he spoke again, but Cassie mimicked him by raising her hand.

"Sir, as you should know, there are many ways to bully. Stating that my work has ever been anything but exemplary is one of those ways. I have not, nor will ever, shirk my responsibilities as a professor at the university. I have gone above and beyond to make sure my curriculum exemplifies the university's standard and that my students know what I taught before they leave my class. I have received accolades from my peers on my studies, teaching, and research. So, for her to make that statement, tells me you are going to try and make me into a bad professor."

The woman started to speak but stopped when Cassie held her hand up again. "I managed to retrieve all my belongings before I left, before you or someone had my office ransacked. Yes, I know. There are people there who still support me. Photos are sitting in my attorney's office while she prepares a case. You pulled my funding and basically pulled my tenure. Now you're attempting to make me look incompetent."

"One, by claiming my work was inferior to university standards and two, by trying to smear my reputation with what I do in my free time away from the university. Say what you will, think what you want, but you will not get away with any of it. Before you decided I wasn't "doing right" you should have talked to me. As it stands now, we have had our last conversation. My attorney will be in contact soon. Enjoy the rest of your evening."

Cassie rose, paused for the effect of how she looked, gave the table a glamorous smile, and sauntered off, greeting other customers as she passed them. She felt her inside lurch yet walked through the crowd like a queen. Making her rounds rather quickly, she then headed to her office.

Drake had seen Cassie as she spoke to table after table. The elegance of Cassie spoke loudly to his soul. He knew she had no interest in him but did his best to daily make her proud of him.

He had seen her at the university they both attended during their freshman year. Taking completely different classes did not allow for chance meetings. He was thrown together with Cassie when they began a dance program together. He learned she was taking it for the exercise, he was taking it for the enjoyment of the art. They both discovered they were quite good and ended up winning several competitions during their college years. They ended up with minor degrees in choreography and dance, as well as their individual majors.

When Cassie had inherited GalUp from her aunt, Drake took one look at it and told her to sell. The place was a defunct, old burlesque hall with dancers that needed to be retired. Cassie must have seen something he didn't, so he followed her lead and took over management of the business for her.

While she was working, he took her plans and helped her get everything in order. The books were well kept, but there were quite a few discrepancies he took upon himself to investigate and correct. Some vendors here and there were giving false invoices and were not too happy about being cut off.

He offered to stay with GalUp while Cassie sought out her dreams of becoming a renowned astrologer. She had talked to him many times regarding her theory about alternate universes. While he personally thought it was bunk, he never discouraged her from following the stars.

Drake knew Cassie was a very astute businesswoman and she learned the burlesque side of the business very quickly. They both had a sharp eye for reading real talent in people and by the end of their first year together, had a show that had become the hit of Texas. People came from every corner of the state to see the shows. By the second year, GalUp had built a reputation for kick butt shows, gorgeous dancers, and had made the entertainment scene across the country, drawing people from every state.

During this time Cassie had built her own reputation as one of the university's leading professors as well as astrologers. She had found new stars, holes, and had many published articles but no proof yet on her theory of a parallel universe. She worked tirelessly to find that proof and was still hunting.

As year five came to them, GalUp had surpassed their wildest dreams of making them a living. When they expanded into dinner as well, things were beyond amazing for them. Cassie had also decided to perform at GalUp weekly. Friday night. While Drake tried to dissuade her, he was also secretly excited to see what she could do and how the crowds would respond.

Her first Friday night, Cassie was a complete nervous wreck. Fumbling around the office, Drake felt she would spaz out and not perform. Little did he know what would happen next. Not ever seeing her practice, Drake didn't know what to expect. The house lights dimmed, a single spotlight was direct dead center stage and Lady Cassandra made her debut.

To say that Cassie captivated the crowd would have been an understatement. As she performed her routines, he watched the crowd literally become enthralled, but when she opened up and sang, he knew Lady Cassandra would be the queen of GalUp. Drake saw a change in her as Cassie appeared on stage. She seemed to settle into herself and at the same time be a different self. The change was subtle and only someone who knew her well would have been able to see it.

Lady Cassandra illuminated the stage. She captured every single eye in the place. She was seductive, sultry, and untouchable. By the time she finished her third song, Drake knew he was her captive. If she never returned the feelings, he would hold her in his heart forever.

Before she left the stage though, Drake saw the subtle change again. And through the years, he watched her develop in this world and in the academic world she longed to be a part of. Her different selves would reveal off and on, and he chalked this up to her personal growth.

He thought her thesis about parallel universes odd and a bit obsessive but listened intently as she worked towards her PhD. One conversation stuck in his mind through the years. As usual, her eyes glowed as she talked through her ideas. She was preparing her final dissertation and wanted it perfect, so she asked him to listen as she read through her final pages.

"I believe we all alternate selves." Cassie began shyly. "Not just here inside, waiting to appear. We have several identities of our nature that are trying to find out who they are also. They live a life parallel to the one we live. Possibly in another universe. Similar but separate and different. One could be the matronly self, just waiting for the time the other selves reach this perfect point. Another could be an adventurer, holding to see if another has decided to take a certain route in life. Do they know each other? That is what we must find out. The existence of parallel and/or multiple universes, as much as it has been explored, is still very much theory. Theory that needs to be proved or disproved. I hope to be able to find an alternative, no, several alternative or parallel universes through my studies of the skies and stars to prove this."

Cassie took a deep breath before speaking again. "I shortened it for you, but that's gist of what I'm presenting."

"Wow, Cass." Was all Drake could think of saying. "That is totally amazing and powerful." And meant it.

Cassie, at this stage in life, had the good graces to blush. She was still very unsure of herself. She had spent almost three years working and proving most of her dissertation. Drake knew she would be broken-hearted if it was not approved.

"Babe." He draped his arm over her shoulder. "They would be fools not to accept this. There's not a shred of unproveable evidence or information in there."

"Oh Drake." Cassie shuddered. "It's so hard to believe it's finally completed. If they don't accept it, what do I do then? I don't have another in me. I so what my PhD."

"Babe." Drake's pet name for Cassie. "I have no doubt it will happen. You spent two years in Australia other countries around the world for your studies. You got this."

Cassie had spent an exhaustive seven years working on the dissertation and when she was accepted, GalUp threw a huge congrats party for her. One of theirs was making it in the world. Cassandra Hunter was now a doctor.

Drake watched her through the years, teaching, dancing, all the while striving to find the answers she wanted for her parallel theory. When she came back from Tennessee, broken-hearted, he wanted to take some snooty people out. For her sake and sanity, he kept his cool and tried to follow her lead. He made a point of sticking close as she met with them after her routine, listening to every word. After she left the table, he introduced himself and gave them their final show for the evening.

"I am going to explain something to you people and want to you understand completely what I am saying to you." He glared at each one of them. "Cassie is not kidding. On Monday morning, her attorney will be contacting the university's legal department. You will be named as the defendant's being sued for defamation and for breach of contract."

Most of the table blanched at this, except for Tyler, who seemed very sure of himself. In fact, so sure, that he let everyone know how smart he thought he was. "Sir," he said, "I have first-hand knowledge that Cassie used the university for monetary gain for this business. She promoted the place all over campus. She has been shamelessly placing cards and handbills everywhere for years. If that is not a breach of contract, I don't what is."

"And just who are you to this university?" Drake asked, but then held his hand up to stop Tyler's response. "Oh wait. Tyler, isn't it?"

Tyler nodded.

"I'm assuming you are some sort of head of department or legal personnel?" Again, Drake held up his hand to Tyler. "Wait. I believe you are an assistant to Dr. Hunter. Someone she should be able to trust with her work. Instead, from what I can ascertain, you have thwarted her ideas since day one. Behind her back."

Tyler attempted to speak again.

"Do not speak unless you have something relevant to say." He charged Tyler. "I handle all the promotions for GalUp. I handle all the business. Nothing is done without my approval. Dr. Hunter comes in once a week to do what she did here tonight. Any promotional items on the campus would be placed there illegally and would be fraudulent. I will make a personal trip there to retrieve those items and make a point of beginning my own suit against someone. And in case you are not aware, 90 percent or more of your staff and students could not afford to step through the doors of GalUp, so it would not benefit anyone employed here to place those."

At this point, Drake was angry all over again at what Cassie was being subjected to and decided to put an end to the whole conversation. "You have until 8 a.m. Monday morning to come to a decision on her tenure. If Dr. Hunter has not heard from you by then in some form, I can guarantee notice from her attorney. I will now leave you to your evening. Enjoy the rest of the performers."

Drake left and made his way upstairs. He looked for Cassie on the floor, but not seeing her, hoped she had gone to the office. Cassie had changed into leggings and an over-sized shirt. To Drake, she looked just as sexy as when she was in her evening dress. She also looked like the girl he had first met years ago. Sitting beside her, he assured her that all would be well, and her dreams would come true.

CHAPTER 4

Cassie woke the next morning, not having any idea what to do with herself, so she decided to put her work in order and see if she could make heads or tails of her last set of research notes. Before becoming fully immersed, she decided to shower, believing this would clean her brain a bit. She had two days to fill before Monday.

Weekends were usually no makeup days, and she usually plaited her hair back before heading out to the closest observatory. Since there would be no observatory this weekend, she would work out of her home office.

As she was finishing the braid, she glanced in the mirror and started at what she saw. Herself, with her hair down, not plaited like she had it now. The odd thing was, this her looked a lot younger.

"Hello." The mirror self spoke.

"I must be having a breakdown." Cassie spoke aloud.

"Why? Are you crazy in your world?"

"Um, who are you?"

"I believe that is quite obvious."

"No, really. I mean, you look like me but you're definitely not a mirror image. Is someone playing tricks to make me look crazy?" She glanced around her bathroom.

"I know our true selves tend to be a little dense at times, but I was hoping to find you a little more open-minded." The mirror Cassie rolled her eyes. "Usually, star people tend to be more open to mirror self-images."

Cassie snorted. "Well, yeah. If the image looking back mirrors them. It's a little creepy seeing me in the mirror looking different than the real me." She shook her head. "Well, that sounded really intelligent."

The mirror Cassie laughed. She shrugged her shoulder as the real Cassie stood there looking dumb founded. Cassie thought to herself. "I don't even remember her mouth actually moving."

"I don't have to speak out loud for you to hear me. And, if I did so, the sound would reverberate off back to me off the mirror and you would just see my lips move."

"Oh good." Cassie snorted. "I'm hearing things as well."

"Look. You're a star gazer. You're open-minded enough to know there is other life in the great beyond." Mirror Cassie gestured to the sky. "What do you dream of? What did you dream of when you were younger?"

Mirror Cassie leaned toward the real Cassie. "I'm the first of your adulthood. The maiden. Carefree, full of dreams, ready to take on the world. This was before you let the world take you over."

Real Cassie stared at Maiden Cassie, not believing her ears or eyes.

"Hey, it's pretty simple really. We've been star gazing since childhood, believing that other life forms, including parallel, live all over the universe. I think you should remember all of that. Have you found evidence yet?"

Cassie nodded positively. "I believe I have but I am temporarily out of commission as far as my star gazing goes, as you put it. Nothing concrete, just hints of things here and there." She shook her head, attempting to clear her mind and thought to herself. "This whole past week must have really got to me. I'm talking to myself, in a mirror. A self that doesn't even look like me. Is this a mental breakdown?"

Maiden Cassie rolled her eyes again, placed her hands on her hips, and gave Cassie the what for as she pointed to a nearby chair waiting for Cassie to take a seat.

"You, myself, are in need of a history lesson. What is happening now is a lifeline laid out for you. What happens in the future will be determined by what you choose in the present and future. Do you remember the day you met Auntie Nev? Do you remember that she talked to you about destiny and that you initially laughed her off?"

"Auntie Nev was searching just like you are now, only she was looking at the outside, nothing on the inside. When you inherited her small fortune, you ran with it. The wild side and the commonsense side worked together. You saw she had started something great but was cut down too soon and didn't dream big enough to see it to the end. You let your hair down a little bit and ran with it. And when your wild side manages to break out, she does amazing things! Well, except for your down time, which a tad boring."

"Wait. Wait. Just wait." Cassie interrupted. "I'm one in the same. I'm not wild. I just know good things when I see them. I also know how to enjoy myself after working all day."

"Do you? I don't see you dating or partying with anyone." Maiden Cassie wiggled her eyebrows. Real Cassie pursed her lips. "I mean, look at Drake. Other than a recent passing hot thought, you haven't given him the time of day. You're all about work." Maiden Cassie twirled, moving so her whole body could be seen. "Now look at me. Hot and ready. What did you do with this me? Studied. Constantly. Did you even get laid when you had the chance?"

"Hold on one second!" Cassie flustered. "I could have. I just didn't feel a quick lay somewhere was worth it. The first time should be special."

"Yeah. That's what Auntie Nev told you and here you are, 45 and squeaky virginal." Maiden Cassie rolled her eyes. "Look, I'm not here to give you a hard time. I'm kind of like the ghost of Christmas past.

I'm your youth. Your dreamer. Before you get to move forward to completion, we must settle some things. Look into your virgin self. Why did you choose to be flirty but not give out? It's not a bad thing, but you're closing yourself off. I see your enchantress all the time, but you suppress her. I can get you the hook-ups, but then you must do the rest. Your enchantress could take you to heights some women never reach if you'd let her. We need to resolve so you can move forward instead of hanging out in limbo."

"But I thought I resolved my wild young self by dancing." She just gazed at herself, younger self, thinking. The Maiden just gazed back then was gone. "No. Wait." Cassie flew to the mirror. "Wait." She cried out, looking hard into the mirror in search of her maiden self.

At that same moment, realization hit her right between the eyes. Cassie just stood in front of the mirror, the conversation playing in her mind. She took a deep, long look at herself. Her now self. Cassie loosened her hair, running her fingers and tousling it. She thought about how she felt Friday night as she danced. Sexy. Sultry. Temptress. "But I didn't do anything." She spoke out loud. "I teased."

"Well girl," another voice filled her thoughts, "Growing up isn't that hard. You're halfway there." She thought she saw something different in the mirror but shook it off. Cassie decided to take her Maiden self out.

Cassie stepped out of her house, dressed for a party. She had hired a driver, knowing she might, big might, need an escort. Her best single, female friend was going to meet her at one of the night clubs on the same block with GalUp. It was the safest place she could think of. At least it wouldn't be full of horny cowboys.

Bella, her best friend, was dressed to seduce. Between the two of them, heads turned. Bella was fair to Cassie's golden hues. Blonde hair, light blue eyes, she drew just as many appraising looks as Cassie.

Years ago, Cassie had bought and converted a taller building on the same block into three different night clubs. The third floor was rock, second floor country, and bottom floor was a jazz type dance club, with office space on the top four floors. Capitalizing her investment was important and upper-scale clubs tended to bring in better clientele and more money than just free entry bars. Three levels offered a little of everything for party goers.

The ladies found a corner table, ordered drinks and chit chatted. Quickly, the players of the night migrated toward their table, elegantly dressed and looking for their next hit of the evening. While Bella took almost every offer to dance, Cassie was a little more reserved, accepting one or two here and there. No drink offers and declining offers to join their table.

Cassie had drunk enough to feel a good buzz and was having fun watching Bella and her entourage. She had just accepted her next drink when a gorgeous, dark-skinned man stepped in her view, requesting a dance. Accepting, she stepped onto the dance floor with him as a slow cheek-to-cheek song began.

The man shrugged, Cassie shrugged, and they danced. Cassie enjoyed his voice as he small-talked her. Until it turned very sultry as he began explaining, in great detail, all the things he planned on doing to her. Cassie stopped moving, told him a polite no, and walked back to her table. He followed. She looked around for Bella but was unable to see her good enough to get her attention. She braced herself as the man leaned in, invading her space.

"I thank you for the dance. I'm not interested in anything further." She spoke, looking for an escape route.

"Ah little one," he crooned, "You came tonight for one thing only."

"Not really." She tried to appear nonchalant. "Just didn't want to sit at home."

"Then you need to be dominated." Grabbing her arm. "I will show you."

"Release me now!" Cassie demanded.

At that moment, an equally seductive voice interrupted. "I would appreciate you releasing her." Cassie felt instant relief.

The man replied. "And I should do this because?"

"Because if you don't, the arm you are touching her with will be forcibly removed, rendered useless, and a scene will close this establishment. Your choice."

The man sized Drake up, deciding it was better to walk away, calling Cassie a filthy name as he did so. Cassie fell against Drake's arm, giggling from relief. "How did you know I was here?"

Sitting her back down and handing her the drink she ordered earlier, he answered. "Security noticed you and called me. Thought I'd come play a bit. Didn't know I was going to have to be your knight in shining armor."

"I could have kicked and screamed. I just didn't want to cause a scene." She giggled again, the adrenaline and alcohol making her feel giddy.

"Next time," he held her chin, looking into her eyes, "make a scene."

Cassie nodded just as Bella returned. "Well, you most certainly do like 'em tall, dark, and handsome. Hey, Drake."

"Bella."

Bella introduced her friend and the four chatted. Drake knew the gentleman. Bella seemed happy. Cassie just felt happy to be left alone. Nothing else was spoken of about the incident and the two couple enjoyed the rest of the evening, dancing, and drinking.

Cassie partnered with Drake and Bella seemed to really be hitting it off with her new guy. By the end of the evening, Cassie was leaning towards not too sober as were the others, so she had the driver take everyone where they wanted, tipping him nicely when she got home, leaving Drake as the final passenger.

As she headed up the steps, Cassie felt a hand on her elbow, steadying her. It was Drake. She felt relieved that he was there and excited at the same time.

"Coffee?" She asked.

"Lots." He replied.

They walked to the kitchen. Cassie had removed her stilettos in favor of bare feet. Drake had removed his jacket and tie. As the coffee percolated, they rummaged through the refrigerator and nibbled bits and pieces of leftover food they managed to find. While Cassie kept rifling in the fridge, Drake stood back watching. Cassie finally stood and smiled shyly as she popped a strawberry and brought one to Drake's mouth. That night, Cassie lost her virginity, and the coffee ended up being good and strong hours later.

Cassie's muscles felt deliciously sore the next morning and she sported a slight headache from the liquor she'd consumed. She stretched and smiled as she thought about the previous night or early morning, remembering each moment with Drake. Smelling freshly brewed coffee, Cassie dressed and padded to her kitchen, taking the cup of coffee Drake offered her.

They spoke in quiet tones that morning, parting when Drake told her he had to go to GalUp for a meeting. Cassie felt something change. but just smiled as he left. She spent the rest of Sunday recuperating, hoping for a phone call, but was left to herself until later that night.

First came the phone call from her attorney, scheduling a meeting for first thing Monday morning with the university. All she would tell Cassie was that things looked interesting. Cassie threw a quick prayer up that she would keep her tenure and be able to complete her research project. Second was a text from Drake telling her not to make plans for the evening, causing her to grin like a silly schoolgirl. And the final contact was an email from an unknown source, "You should know that you will be losing GalUp if you let this deal go through."

Cassie immediately texted Drake to contact her ASAP, which he did. She explained the text, then demanded answers. He told her to calm down and that he would talk to her later.

"No, Drake." She exclaimed. "That is my place. I want to know what's going on."

"Cass," he sighed, "I'm in a meeting right now. We'll talk later."

"Drake." She called into the phone and heard nothing but dead air.

Scared and mad, Cassie dressed comfortably business-like in something suitable for a meeting and headed to GalUp. She entered from the rear quietly, wanting to know who Drake was meeting with. As she started up the stairs, Cassie heard voices coming from the small conference room next to the small staff kitchen. She heard Drake in a heated discussion with two other voices and then heard a female voice break in.

"It's for the good of the company. We don't need any more liabilities. If this thing breaks, it could cost us a lot of money."

Cassie stiffened, wondering what company there were talking about being in trouble, knowing it was about GalUp somehow.

"The stockholders heard about the incident at the university, and they feel that if the upcoming meeting with the potential new business doesn't go well or the wrong information gets out, profits will plummet." The woman continued. Cassie wondered how they had heard about the meeting so fast.

Drake sounded ticked, which made Cassie's nerves tingle. "That little prick, Tyler, can be shut down. He'd be the only one to keep stirring up trouble."

Now Cassie was totally engrossed and peeved. She knew this was the stockholders trump card and one of the reasons she had never wanted to go public. She still had controlling interest so they could do much but complain. She hoped.

Drake continued. "Let's wait to see how tomorrow works out, then we'll take the next step. I don't see cause for concern at present."

"No." The woman stubbornly replied. "We need to decide a course of action now, before something happens."

On of the male voices spoke. "What if she's asked not to make an appearance until the university decision is rendered?"

"What about, no." Drake responded. "The two have never met, never been exposed to each other. I see no reason to do so. It is a punishment for no reason."

"Doesn't matter. Now they have met. The people from the university were here and saw her perform. It wasn't just the lower administration, it was the prefects, Drake." One man spoke. "Look, it's a simple request. Just for a while. Let things calm down, then she can choose whichever if the university lets her return."

Cassie, hearing enough, flung the door wide open, startling the room. "There will be no choosing." Walking to the table, "What the hell, Drake! When were you going to let me know about this?"

Drake stood.

"No. Just no. I'm not stupid enough to believe this is all coincidence. That little SOB is now trying another route to crush me." Cassie leaned across the table and grabbed the revenue folder. "Revenue is still high. In fact, better than ever. Not because I dance or don't, no one knows I own it, but because this place is unique. We offer something for everyone. That's the draw, not me."

"The university and GalUp will never meet. I have and always will make sure of that. What happens with them is none of your concern. None. You want me out, you better make damn sure to have a good reason or a better attorney." Turning to Drake, Cassie poked his chest. "Don't bother coming over tonight. I won't be there." And stormed out of the room, leaving them all staring in the direction she left.

Drake turned back to the table. "Well, there you have it. As I told you, this could have waited. It's not that she's not predictable now, it's that she's pissed, and this is out of my hands."

Now he had to find Cassie, which wasn't going to be easy. He knew she'd stay close because of her meeting in the morning. The question was, where? Three hours later, it dawned on him where she would go.

As he drove up the drive to her Auntie's small ranch, though no lights were on, Drake knew Cassie was there. He didn't go inside but around to the barn.

"You remembered." He heard as he walked up to it. He looked up to see Cassie sitting on the deck she had built for her stargazing. She was looking at the sky.

"Yeah. It took a while." He replied. "I almost forgot about this place. May I come up?"

"Sure, why not. My life has been completely invaded. What's one more spot."

Drake kept silent even though the remark was hurtful, knowing it wasn't totally directed at him He made his way up. Cassie saw Drake and smiled, knowing he cared, but wouldn't talk until she was ready to. His presence was comforting and helped calm her even more than this place or the stars.

"All I ever wanted was to go to the stars. Find proof out there. Find the parallel worlds that so many believe in." She paused. "There can't be just so much nothing."

Drake kept silent, letting her muse and work things out.

"I always thought to be an astronaut, but then became captivated by finding stars. Are there life forms on them? Are there other earths but with different versions of ourselves? There is universe upon universe. How do I find them?"

Cassie stood and walked to the huge telescope, peering through the lens. "When I got the inheritance, maybe I should have taken it and run. But GalUp was something of a challenge, which I like, and it gave me financial freedom. I loved Auntie Nev and didn't want to lose her twice. Now look what it has become. Why do people hate dreamers so much? I earned my PhD. I earned GalUp. Now everyone wants to take them away from me." She stated flatly. "I just need for one dream to come true."

Drake came up behind her and enveloped her in his arms. "Babe, no one's taking anything. It's all very far up in the air. You're just on a temporary pause. Relax. Take some time for you."

"No." She broke away. "I got funded for this. I was trusted. Now it's gone. Can't get it back no matter how hard I try. Now I get the pleasure of proving my theory without the support of the university. Doesn't sit well with me."

Drake knew reasoning would not help at this point with the funk that Cassie was in. "Come to the kitchen. I've not eaten all day. I know you just had the pantry stocked." He left and walked towards the house.

Cassie watched him go, saw the lights blink on, and Drake through the window exploring and gathering things. She wasn't quite ready to give in, so she returned to her chair. Breathing to calm herself, Cassie heard a voice speaking very clearly. Looking around and seeing no one, she leaned forward checking for Drake, who she could see was still in the kitchen.

"Officially," she giggled, "looks like insanity might be creeping in."

"Girl," the voice spoke, "no insanity."

"Who?"

"I'm you, sort of." The voice was hers, just, well, very throaty. Kind of sexy. "That man there has devoted his whole life to you. He's watched and helped you become the woman you are today. Did you know you were his first as well?"

Cassie gasped, "No!"

"We've met before you and I. When you're on the dance floor, I can fill you and bring your seductress out."

Cassie shuddered, really wondering if she was losing her mind.

"No, you're not crazy, just growing. Your virgin self helped you through school and achieving your goals. She kept you focused, pure, and goal oriented. I kept you hot." The voice laughed at this, Cassie did not.

"So, you're me also, just the slut part?" Cassie queried.

"Humph." The voice snorted. "You'll figure it out but never a slut."

"Then who are you?" But received no answer. "Hello?"

Cassie looked around but saw nothing or no one. She questioned but received no answer. She quickly gathered herself and headed to her auntie's house, well, technically her house and the safety of Drake. He had an amazing dinner/breakfast laid out. It was close to 1 a.m. and he had made a brunch style meal.

Again, they talked little, each deep in their thoughts but completely aware of each other. They cleaned the kitchen together and went to the den, settling on the oversized sofa to watch TV. Drake stretched his arms across the back of the soft and within minutes, Cassie snuggled into him, and within a few minutes more, both fell asleep.

A gentle nudge woke Cassie the next morning, along with the wonderful smell of hot coffee. "It's time to go, babe." Drake smiled down at her. "The meeting is in two hours. Time for the next song and dance."

Cassie moaned loudly as she stretched her cramped muscles. Although she enjoyed the way she fell asleep, her body didn't. Sipping from the mug of coffee, she stood and stretched more as Drake watched appreciatively.

"If you knew." Drake muttered.

"Knew what?" She asked.

This pulled Drake from his musing, and he fumbled for words. "Knew how much I hate not showering in the morning."

"The utilities are on." Cassie informed him, missing Drake's innuendo completely.

"No fresh clothes." He replied. "Let's go. One car or two?"

"I'll go solo. I hate being stuck."

With that and Drake feeling tense, they left for the city, each making a quick trip to their apartments, promising to see each other at the attorney's office.

CHAPTER 5

Cassie arrived first after a quick wash and change. She wanted a few minutes with her attorney before the circus began. Cassie had decided to try and buy the outstanding shares, if any, of GalUp and unsuccessfully got that out of the way before everyone showed up. Vespa, her attorney didn't find any available and promised to see what she could find. Drake had shown up ten minutes before the university people.

The university brought three attorneys, the dean, Cassie's prefect, and Tyler. How he managed that was anybody's guess, but there he was. Once in the conference room, as sides were taken, the games began. One of the university attorneys began, but Drake quickly broke in.

"I don't see a need for this man," pointing to Tyler, "to be here."

"Sir, it's his father's law firm and being unable to attend, he sent his son."

"What does Tyler's being here have to do with Dr. Hunter's position?"

"Not that it's any of your concern, but he is here in his father's stead. We do as he requests."

Drake leaned back, shaking his head and the attorney began again.

"As we, the university, see things, Dr. Hunter holds a second job," saying this with distaste, "that affects the university. She therefore must make the decision as to which one is more important."

Cassie started out of her chair, Vespa, attorney motioned her to sit. "Let them say their piece."

"It is the university's contention that she uses her position here to promote her work there. While it is admirable of her to hold two positions, it's the type of work outside of the university that has brought about this issue. The university upholds strict morals on what our professors should be like in their off time. Working at a burlesque bar is not how we desire our students to see their professors. Promotion of a business like this should not be done in a place of higher learning."

Cassie started, again her attorney motioned her down.

"We note her extracurricular activities are hers, but they endanger her position with the university. Here are our terms:

1. Cease and desist all campus advertising, oral, online, and written.
2. Reduce teaching hours to be more focused on course specific classes.
3. Do not work at second position on days teaching.
4. Dress appropriately for a professor of this university.
5. Turn over all materials and funds for the project the university funded.

If the university at any time feels these guidelines are not being met, tenure will be revoked. You have lost funding for your project and will be allowed campus work only. You will not tutor privately nor be allowed to take student off campus for any reason."

At this point, Drake stood, ready to do battle, but like Cassie, the attorney motioned him to be seated. She let silence hover in the air as she turned each page slowly, making notes as she did. Cassie even thought there was a harumph once or twice in there. At the last page, the attorney wrote something on her pad with a flourish, closed the binder, laid her pen down and flung the binder in the trash.

The whole room gasped, and the university attorneys looked indignant. "You can't do that!" The first one exclaimed.

"Seems to me I just did."

He stood. She told him to sit down. "That's got to be one of the biggest, stupidest pieces of crap I've laid eyes on in years. Sit!"

Vespa Duncan stood at 6'3. She was half Italian, half Scots and greatly favored in looks from her Italian side. Verbally, she had a Scottish brogue with a hint of an Italian accent. Temper-wise, let's just say Scots and Italian had make her a very volatile person. She knew she could stop traffic with her looks but chose to stop crime instead. Vespa was destined to be a judge. Vespa flipped to the last of her notes and flipped the pad so the other side could see. "NO." Laying the pad down, she returned to her chair and crossed her long legs.

"One, at no time in the last 20 or so years has my client ever promoted herself or GalUp at the university. Prove that she has. Two, she will not reduce hours. There is not a more focused prof withing the walls of that place. Three, she can work at GalUp any day she desires, but she has actually only ever worked on Fridays. Four, I've only ever seen her in suits. What is not appropriate with that? Five, the morals clause in her contract with the university reads way different than you are implying. Six, her project was hers before funding so just a big fat No to that. Period. We anticipated you wanting your funds returned." She flung an envelope across to the table. "Here's the remaining funds with an itemized expenditure of the funds not returned."

Tyler leaned to speak to the university attorney. They spoke for a couple of minutes before Vespa broke in. "Sorry to disturb your little party. May I be allowed to finish?"

The attorney smirked at Vespa. "Please, Ms. Duncan.

"Seems to me, you have placed Dr. Hunter under censorship. But, before we get into any more particulars, let me weave a little story for you. And I'm a great storyteller." Vespa paused, steepled her fingers, then loudly cracked them, causing note-worthy cringing around the room.

"Riddle me this. When you're a star athlete trying to keep your head above water, how do you do that? Find a way to make things change. Spread a little money around, do a little favor here and there. Before I go any further, does anyone have any confessions to make? Off the record, of course." Vespa directed a piercing glare towards Tyler who was keeping his eyes glued to something in his lap.

"No? Then let's continue. I'm excited to know the ending." Vespa giggled and clapped her hands. "So, let's look at this picture. Our young star athlete is failing his classes. One of them, he is required to do a research dissertation to pass. Now this fellow has managed to get his grades just above passing in all his classes but astronomy. Wonder how? He decides to travel a different path to achieve his goals. His prof, who is quite the looker, is looking for an assistant to help with her work and it will involve some travel. He signs up, proclaiming it will help him with his grades. And low and behold, the prof accepts his explanation."

Tyler is now glaring at Cassie, who glares back. Drake sees where this is going and feels himself flush with anger.

"Our star athlete is very accommodating with his help, seemingly hanging on the prof's every word as she works. He knows he has to do something to get the grade raised or daddy won't be happy. Late one evening, the next to last week of their journey, our star athlete decides it's time to make some type of move on her. After coming on rather strongly to the prof, being rejected rather forcefully, if you knee what I mean, our star athlete took to tapping the prof's phone. Cad."

"One phone call in particular, gave him an idea and a piece of knowledge he used against the prof to make her look like a slut. In his lower extremities where his brain resides, that's what she was. Our star athlete carefully wove his trashy novel, taking it to daddy to make sure it would work. Daddy made sure to dot the Is and cross the Ts and cut our star athlete loose."

"But our fella forgot one thing. Evidence. First, evidence that the prof was what he was claiming. None. Just his word. Evidence of use of her job to promote GalUp. None. For years. None. Second, covering his evidence of tapping her phone. While there were calls to and from her, there's a particular ping that shows an outside tap. Oops! Evidence that he paid or did other favors for his other profs to get a better grade. I mean, what physics prof can afford, cash sale, a new Benz. What electronic assistant can just, all of the sudden, get a major electronic system in his apartment? Oops!"

Tyler was flushed an embarrassing shade of red, Drake was blazing pissed off red, Cassie was furious, as well as the university's attorney being disgustedly angry. Tension was very heavy and high in the room.

The university attorney decided the cool approach, knowing that he had been lied to, just to test the waters. "If, big if, what you say might be remotely true, why would this star athlete risk his reputation for a stripper?"

Vespa snickered, holding her hand once again to Cassie and Drake. She knew this game, hated it, wasn't going for it. "Okay. Okay. I see where this is going. But let me assure you, if this is the route you want to travel, your star athlete, his daddy, the other profs, the university, and you will wish you never traveled it."

Vespa pressed the intercom, and an intern brought in a box. Vespa pulled a couple of folders out as well as a disc she put in her computer. "First, I would appreciate you reviewing the contents of your folders. Should you question the contents, I will then move to share the video which will put pretty boy here into the light of day."

As the university attorneys sifted through page after page of pictures and comments of the staff at Tennessee, then shared them with the dean and prefect, leaving Tyler out, the lead attorney placed the folder in his briefcase and spoke. "While this material is enlightening, it still does not explain why Dr. Hunter feels it necessary to strip at night. The university frowns on this type of extracurricular activity. Someone her age should act more responsible and respectful."

"My age!" Cassie shouted.

"Dr. Hunter's age has nothing to do with this, first off. Secondly, it's not stripping, it's burlesque, meaning with clothes. Thirdly, one night a week she does one set, then she's done. Next, as has been previously stated, the people that can afford to attend these shows certainly are not college students, hence, the twain have no chance of meeting. Finally, again," this word being heavily stressed, "nowhere in the morals section does it state anything about certain "extracurricular activities," air quotes, "being frowned upon."

"If you wish to pursue any of this, let's begin. I expect undeniable evidence, proof, that it's affecting the university financially as well as attendance-wise. Proof that her students are failing her classes. Proof of her ineptitude as a teacher, complaints filed against her, and evidence she has misused her position to further GalUp. I would also like evidence that she has misappropriated any funds that were awarded to her for her research. You have 30 days to produce this. If you have not or cannot produce this, I expect all accusations to be dropped and forgotten. In the meantime, Dr. Hunter will continue to teach her classes as she sees fit, without restrictions, conditions, or questions. Just as if nothing ever happened."

"If you just happen to find enough evidence to warrant moving forward, be assured, I will hang all of you out to dry for false accusations, defamation, and pretty much whatever else I decide to use. If one iota of this leaks out to students, faculty, news media, or anyone related to the university, causing any form of hardship to Dr. Hunter, you will wish it was only defamation of character I was charging. Your star athlete will not be allowed near Dr. Hunter and will transfer all his classes with her to another prof. Today. Should this person decide to start trouble, we will go after everyone."

"Gentlemen, lady," Vespa stood and leaned over the table in their direction, show a good amount of cleavage as well as a threatening glare, "Money may solve a lot of problems in your little part of the world, but in mine, it just starts them. I have very good friends in the media who are looking for the next "big story." And the picture I can paint..." She trailed off then continued. "Is that the picture you want?"

The dean stood, motioning to his side of the table. All stood, preparing to leave. He spoke. "Be assured Ms. Duncan, this matter will be investigated thoroughly. I am not pleased that Dr. Hunter is to remain, but at present, we have no recourse. It was not proper that she was dismissed in the fashion she was. I will address that with the board. We will have a response for you within 30 days." He began leaving and turned at the door. "The research funding shall not be returned. It has been rescinded by the grantor." With that, he left the room.

Both Cassie and Drake turned back to Vespa full of questions. She smiled, threw one of her folders to them and waited as the group left the room. As soon as the door closed, questions were thrown at her with lightning speed. She held her hands up in a plea of mercy, smiling like a cat that ate the canary. Once Cassie and Drake quieted, Vespa explained.

"Now I know you didn't get your funding back. Nothing I can really do there. The foundation has Tyler's dad on the board, so I'll leave it at that." Cassie started to speak. "Just wait, doll." Vespa told her.

"You've at least got 30 days right now to make decisions about your future. You're still teaching. Hopefully, this time off has helped your class, not hurt, so it will probably be full when you go in tomorrow. As far as anyone knows, you just returned from your trip. Make your presentation about that good."

"Here's the next moves. They will send interrogatories, which we'll answer. They will delve into your personal life, so be prepared. They will delve into your, how'd they say it, extracurricular activities, which we'll answer. When we are done, the judge will think you're a saint. If we get that far."

Cassie couldn't stand being silent any longer. "But how will my research be completed? That's why I was in Tennessee. I need to finish."

"Babe." Drake put a hand on hers.

"No! I could use my money, but the point of backers from the university is to prove that someone besides me believes in my research. Am I just supposed to teach for the rest of my career?" Cassie was close to tears.

"Cassie," Vespa sympathized, "We've known each other forever. You're tough. Find another grant. Beat these morons at their own game. At least you're still there and not on leave. Look, let's start here. We'll be in weekly contact for sure. Go on with life as if nothing's happened. One step at a time."

With the meeting over, they all went for brunch just to get chilled and on track. Cassie left alone and drove, then wound up back at her townhouse, preparing for her classes the next day. She left a message on her phone stating as much and shut it off. Later that evening as she showered, she found herself gazing into the mirror again but saw only herself. Nothing different. Well, a little different. Weariness was etched around her eyes, and she felt it beating against her determination. She nodded and gave up the night.

CHAPTER 6

"Girl." A voice woke Cassie.

"It's 4 a.m. what the hell!" Cassie moaned.

"Haul it up, girl." The voice spoke again. "You'll be up in 30 minutes anyway. Come on, sis. I don't have much longer."

With that, Cassie bolted awake, looking around her bedroom. "Is someone here?"

"Well of course someone is. Listen, got to tell you something before I walk."

Cassie threw herself out of bed, tripped but managed to land in a chair close by.

"Take it easy. Just sit and relax. We can talk here." Cassie knew it was her Maiden self and now really felt like she was insane or heading in that direction.

"No, you're not insane. You're searching and perfectly normal. If it helps, turn your mirror around."

Cassie did. The small one she left on her reading table. She immediately saw the Maiden version of herself. She hadn't changed one bit.

"Look," Maiden Cassie said, "this parallel universe thing is cool and potentially true. Can't say yea or nay, but not why I'm here."

"Then why are you here? I'm not quite comprehending why I'm seeing me, but not me." Cassie questioned.

"I'm here to say goodbye and let you know that you're on the right track. Sort of."

"Okay. That really cleared things up."

"Girl," Maiden Cassie leaned forward and rolled her eyes, "I'm not an airhead and neither are you, so quit insulting us. My time is short, and I really need to share with you."

Cassie leaned back and threw her hands up in defeat.

"Now, you did good with Drake. That's a sweet piece of candy. Just follow through with that one. Yummy!"

Cassie rolled her eyes this time. "Move along."

"I'm just saying." Maiden Cassie said, causing Cassie to glare at her. "Okay, okay. Listen. There is life out there." Pointing skyward. "You know it. Proving it, difficult. Look within to look without. Once you get that and I mean really understand what it means, you'll find all your answers. I feel myself fading." Maiden Cassie grimaced. "Look you, don't let anyone conform you like they're trying to. You got played, and you know that, by that little scum sucker and his daddy."

"Now, you have to show them who's the bomb. Everyone is going to ask you to stop your nightlife. Don't. It does define you, even if it's one night a week. If they steal that from you, they win. Girl, believe it or not, the you you're becoming will shake the world. Be open, be virginal, be amazing. Love yourself first. You know the stars, now show the stars. You will figure this all out. Gotta go. Ciao."

And with that, the mirror stood empty. Cassie saw twinges of dawn and just stared, watching the sky change. She had never felt as sure about her life as she did at that very moment but confused at the same time.

As expected, her classroom was at full capacity. She scanned the students, making sure Tyler wasn't hiding out and noticed a regent seated in a corner. She acknowledged him, he did likewise to her. The class couldn't have gone better. She talked about her research and fielded questions. An hour and a half later, she stood looking across the empty theater not seeing the regent standing off to her side. He cleared his throat, bringing her out of her daze.

"Yes, sir." Cassie acknowledged.

"I do not know why I was asked to review your class today, but I will say it was quite interesting. I see no reason to review again, Dr. Hunter. Well done."

Cassie smiled and nodded, gathered her things, and went to her office. An envelope was attached to her door. It read:

"Dr. Hunter,

It has come to my attention that the funding for your research has been rescinded. Please find enclosed a check for the balance rescinded, and an additional sum for your inconvenience, and unlimited use of any of the observatories in Texas. You already have the paperwork completed and on file, copies are enclosed, as well as accounting ledgers for your expenses. We are impressed with your work and look forward to your final reports. Please forward weekly reports to address enclosed."

And that was it. Cassie could find no clue as to who had sent it. No one had seen any of her research. Cassie was ecstatic and phoned Drake, getting his voice mail. In 24 hours, her upside-down world had tilted a little toward the positive side. Or so she thought.

As she completed her work for the day and was preparing to head out, her office phone rang. "I know what you are, trash." Click. Cassie just stared at the phone, tried to reverse the call, got nothing. It rang again, she sent it to voice mail so the time and call would be documented. No one mentioned for her to do this, but prudence told her to gather any evidence she could.

As she left the department, she felt like someone was watching her but couldn't see anything unusual. There was a note on her car, computer printed. "I know what you are, whore."

She calmly placed the note in her bag and locked herself in her car. After making her deposit, Cassie chose home over GalUp, needing the comfort of her space there. But it was not to be had either because another printed note was attached to her door with the same message.

Now pissed, she left a voice mail for Vespa and Drake, telling them she would be in her safe place, knowing Drake knew that place and Vespa would call Drake first. Cassie loaded all her research, food, clothes, and anything she thought necessary into the Rover in her garage, waiting for the cover of dark. She didn't know if anyone was watching her and wasn't taking any chances.

A few hours later, after several detours, she pulled up to her ranch house. She shut the lights off and watched for a few minutes to see if any lights came up the road or up her drive. Two hours later, settled in, she phoned Drake again, left no message, and went to her front porch. She loved the ranch and the wholeness she felt of being there. Her phone rang. Drake.

"Babe," using his nickname for her. "What the hell is going on?"

Cassie filled him in, telling him where she hid the notes for him and Vespa.

"You need company?"

"Not tonight."

"Call me before you leave for town tomorrow."

"I will."

Cassie leaned back and listened to the quietness. It was calming. Her mind was not. She dozed and dreamed. A soft, seductive voice woke her. Cassie knew immediately it was herself, but not which one until the voice spoke again.

"Honey, let's get this show on the road. Wake up. As the old saying goes, 'We're burnin' daylight.' Get your coffee, let's chat."

Cassie went to her bedroom after pouring the coffee she'd set up to brew earlier. She found another standup mirror in the bath on settled by the window, placing the mirror on the small table there. "Hello me." Cassie mumbled. "Little early for this crap."

"You're such a morning person. You have to leave in a couple of hours so thought I'd re-introduce myself." Enchantress Cassie smiled at Cassie.

Cassie mumbled back at the mirror. Enchantress Cassie seemed to exude sex appeal and confidence. "Listen woman, you've been blessed beyond measure in the last couple of days. Things are looking up, aren't they?"

Another mumble.

"Cass, you're 45. You've got the careers you've always wanted, a man, finally, and you're set for retirement. I'm feeling that you seem to think you're at a crossroads here."

"You think." Cassie snarked.

"Look, you're teaching again. Comfy, cozy. Are you happy? You got your research, the money you need to continue. What are you going to do when that's over?"

Cassie just started at her mirror image. "I'm here. Thinking of selling the townhouse. Isn't that something?"

"Again, something comfortable."

"Well, since I can now work on my research again, proving my parallel theory is back in the works. Some travel." Cassie offered.

"It's a start." Enchantress Cassie replied. "But what about tall, dark, and utterly gorgeous? You've had one wonderful, sexy night. I'm feeling kind of itchy now. What's up with that?"

Cassie knew she had been avoiding Drake the last few days, but she needed time to examine her feelings. She knew Friday would come fast and she'd see him then but needed to understand herself and what happened between them. They were deep, dear friends and she didn't want to lose that. Cassie harrumphed.

"Listen," Enchantress Cassie's voice became stern. "You've got a lot to look forward to. I'm not here for kicks. You need to look within to find what you're looking for out there."

This perked Cassie up as she had heard something similar from the first Cassie. "Why did you say that? She asked her mirrored self. "I heard it from another recently."

"Then you should listen. You, we, search for the unknown. But perhaps the unknown is what's inside of us that we don't know about yet. Maybe that's the universe that should be explored." Enchantress Cassie had a faraway look now. "When you search the stars, searching for life, parallel, remember what you heard. In the meantime, get laid again. You're not getting any younger and Drake is good." And then the Enchantress was gone, leaving Cassie to herself.

"Well, crap." She sighed, seeing the light of dawn. "Now what?" And rose to prepare for the day.

CHAPTER 7

The first week back to teaching was mostly uneventful. Friday, a couple of notes appeared again, which she got to Vespa before heading to the club. Drake was not to be found, which gave her concern, but she had come to dance, so she did.

She was feeling sultry so had Thomas pop a sexy hard, sexy sass and instead of her singing, pulled a song designed to seduce. She needed to release some pent-up energy. Dark green suited her again tonight. Everything she did with makeup and costume enhanced her face and body. She was a total seductress. Cassie felt the sexiest she had ever felt in her life as she headed to the stage. She knew eyes were watching as she placed herself on the rising platform. When the music started, smoke swirled, and she began her set.

The room was hushed, the air thick with anticipation. A single, muted spotlight bathed the center of the stage, where a raised platform began to rise slowly from beneath the floor. Cassie stood poised, a figure of sultry confidence, her body barely visible beneath the low glow. The soft, haunting notes of a violin drifted through the room, weaving a spell of intrigue. The audience held its collective breath, drawn into the quiet allure.

The platform reached stage level, and for a heartbeat, everything was still. The violin faded, replaced by a low, pulsing bass, steady, rhythmic, like the calm before a storm. Then it happened... a sharp, electrifying drumbeat shattered the silence. On that beat, Cassie *exploded* into motion, and the room was set ablaze.

Cassie was dressed to kill. A black leather bralette hugged her torso, adorned with gold accents that caught the stage lights. High-waisted shorts, equally black and shimmering, revealed long, toned legs wrapped in crisscrossing gold straps. Over this, she wore a cropped leather jacket, which she would peel off at just the right moment. Her stilettos were fierce, glossy black with gold heels, elevating her every move.

A bold choker encircled her neck, and her wrists glinted with matching cuffs. Her hair was wild and tousled, a deliberate mix of power and seduction, framing her smokey-eyed gaze that pierced through the dim lighting.

The music was relentless. A driving beat pulsed through the room, layered with electronic synths and the wailing edge of an electric guitar. The tempo was fast, aggressive, and impossible to ignore. It was the kind of track that demanded movement, rebellion, and power, a perfect storm of sexy and savage.

Cassie's body moved with fierce precision, every motion sharp and deliberate. She threw her arms out, snapping her head to the side as her hips hit the beat with a mesmerizing sway. Her stilettos struck the stage like thunderclaps as she marched to the front, her eyes locking onto the crowd, daring them to look away.

She slid into a low squat, rolling her hips with serpentine grace, then sprung up with explosive energy. The leather jacket slid off her shoulders, falling to the stage in one fluid motion, revealing the full power of her form. She strutted across the stage with authority, each step a statement.

Cassie used the stage like her personal battlefield, owning every inch of it. She leaned into the music, her body twisting and turning in sync with the pounding bass. She spun sharply, her hair whipping around her like a fierce halo, before dropping to her knees and arching backward, her chest rising as her hands glided along her thighs.

Cassie stepped forward with a powerful stomp, her heel hitting the stage with a satisfying crack. She turned sharply on her heel, executing a flawless pivot as she flipped her hair over her shoulder, throwing a sultry glance at the crowd.

She grabbed a stage prop, a slender cane decorated with shimmering gold and used it as an extension of her body. Twirling it above her head, she let it whip around her, striking the floor in rhythm with the beat. She lifted it, balancing it on her shoulders, rolling her hips in a slow, tantalizing circle.

As the music shifted into a deeper, grittier rhythm, Cassie dropped low and crawled forward, her body undulating like a predator stalking its prey. Her eyes were fixed on the crowd, her movements deliberate and intense, each step a calculated strike of power and allure.

Rising onto her knees, she arched backward, tossing her head so her hair swept the floor in a wild, untamed motion. The lights caught her glistening skin, highlighting every curve as she moved with unrelenting energy.

As the music crescendos into its final, intense sequence, Cassie's moves become a frenzy of hard, fast-paced choreography. She launches into a rapid series of spins, her arms slicing through the air with perfect precision. She leaps, landing in a split, before rising seamlessly into a high kick that sends her stilettos slicing through the air.

The lights flashed wildly, casting her in sharp colors as she pounded the stage with every beat. She turned sharply toward the center of the stage, gripping the cane once more, and raised it high above her head. With the final drumbeat, she slammed the cane down with all her force, and the lights go black.

For a moment, there is only silence. Then the lights rose again, revealing Cassie standing center stage, her chest rising and falling as she stared out at the mesmerized audience. A smirk played on her lips, and she threw one final, slow wink before the stage went dark again.

As the beat of her third song ended, the hall detonated with applause and cheers. No one was left in their seats as she made her bow and exit. The applause was still heard as Cassie walked up to her office. Nods of approval were received as she passed the other dancers. Cassie dropped into the chair in front of her makeup table, calming her breathing and swigging water.

"Well, well, well." A familiar voice commented.

Cassie looked up, seeing herself in the mirror. Technically her Enchantress self. "What gives? Did you come out tonight?" She asked her enchantress self.

"Baby doll," Enchantress Cassie sniggered, "tonight was all you. And I have to ask, where in the devil did that come from?"

Cassie just grinned. "It came, that's all I know."

"I'm impressed. You set some people on fire tonight."

Cassie cleaned her face, needing to become her normal self for some reason. She suddenly felt the urge to star gaze.

Enchantress Cassie leaned close to the mirror. "Remember to mark what you see tonight. Stars never lie."

Cassie escaped GalUp as fast as she could, heading to her ranch and her telescope. Not as strong as she wished, she'd contact Rafe's tomorrow to see if they would let her come. As she gazed around the sky, she spotted her same olds, but then thought she saw some sort of anomaly and scanned back and forth, making sure to note the coordinates. Her phone rang, she ignored it, still scanning, searching for that... whatever it was she saw. Now there was nothing. But if she could get to a real scope, she might have better luck. Picking up her notes and phone, she automatically dialed back the number. Drake.

"Hey babe." His husky voice warmed her heart and body.

"Hey." She replied. "Was onto something and didn't want to be bothered."

He didn't ask for an explanation, knowing it was the sky that captured her. "Heard you closed the show down tonight."

Cassie smiled.

"I was tied up with a stockholder who came to town. Sorry." He had seen Cassie's performance and was stunned at the feelings it provoked but knew he had to let her talk about it or things.

"Yeah. Well, it's been a week. I needed the exercise. I didn't think it was one of my better sets." She knew better but wasn't fishing for compliments, she was still in her star/sky mode.

"Hon," Drake drawled out, "the girls after you worked their tails off to match you. Your tip jar had over $3,000 in it."

Cassie was stunned at that comment. "Really?" She stopped, spotting the "thing" in the sky again. Scribbling notes furiously by the light of her cell phone, forgetting Drake until she finished, then hearing his voice again.

"Babe? Cass? You there?" He sounded worried.

"No. Yes, I'm here. Had to make a note of something. Sorry." She began walking towards the house again. "Drake, split the tips between the girls. Tell them I appreciate everything they do."

Drake had already done so, knowing Cassie would have done the same if she had stuck around. Knowing Cassie had no idea of the current time, he replied. "Will do." Then asked, "Will you be coming to town tomorrow?"

"No. Can't. Going to Rafe's tomorrow, Drake. I got a lead on something. I need to check it asap." She couldn't get her mind into the phone call. "I'll call you when I get back." And hung up.

Drake had learned not to break her concentration and accepted that she had hung up on him. He knew she had been acting distant since their night together and wanted to get to the bottom of that. The notes were another matter. He thought he knew who was sending them but having her followed had resulted in nothing. Maybe next week would be better. Whoever was stalking Cassie knew her routine well. Now it was a matter of catching the SOB. As he drove home, he also thought about the business at hand with GalUp. Some of the shareholders were demanding more money be made with the conglomerate it was becoming. The area catered to everything but strippers.

With all the various businesses and with one space still open, they wanted it to become a strip/gentleman's club so that those who couldn't afford GalUp could have a place a little less costly to go. To them, it made sense. To him and especially Cassie, it made them trashy. While they both understood why most women stripped, the disadvantage was the type of people clubs like that attracted.

Drake had managed this battle quite well up until the mismanagement of stockholder shares and now was fighting for the life of the area. The battle lines had been drawn, now the war had to be fought. He had to find a money-making business for that space and fast. It needed to be a good income maker and one of a kind. Holding off the stockholders was the challenge. Talking to Cassie about it was going to be an even bigger challenge.

He let his tired but wired mind rest when he arrived at his home, checking Cass's townhouse on the way, sipped some good strong chamomile tea and slept like the dead. With the weekend came rest, normally. He knew Cassie was probably headed to one of the observatories, lost in her theory, happy she was working again. He still wanted to talk with her but was afraid it would be too late after her time with the sky.

A phone call at seven in the morning changed his whole day. "Vespa." He answered.

"We got trouble." She warned.

His hackles rose as Vespa explained about an article she read in a small gazette. "Headline: Stars to Stilettos. Local professor moonlights as a stripper."

"Shit, shit, shit." Drake spit out. "Where is this paper from?"

"Little community not far from the university." Vespa answered. "A lot of the alum live in the area, including our star athlete's father."

"Holy crap!" He exclaimed. "So, their little paper just happened to dig this info up on Cassie?"

"Looking that way." Vespa confirmed. "Or got it from Tyler. And on the weekend as well. I can't reach a soul there to get it retracted. Gonna be a long 48 hours."

Drake was completely pissed. The battle just got bigger. Sides were being drawn and this was just the first week. "What about driving there with a cease and desist?"

"Already sent one with a note of retraction demand as well as a statement." Vespa answered. "It won't pull what's already done but will stop future editorials. Whoever did this knows how to start shit." Vespa did not sound happy. "They're going to set her up to fire her. As long as we keep it off campus, things will be fine. Did you find anything on the letters?"

They chatted and discussed the events of the week and possibilities of the next three weeks. It was also decided not to tell Cassie until they knew the whys and wheres. She knew about the notes, that was enough. If it looked like things were going to escalate, they would fill her in.

Drake headed to the club. He could direct better from there. He wanted to check out the new girls as well, see if they met GalUp standards. The cleaning staff had done their job well but looked like they dropped a box on their way out. As Drake picked it up, he saw Cassie's name scrawled across one side and dread filled him.

In his office, he carefully opened the package. "No explosions." He breathed out, feeling foolish for speaking out loud. A disc fell out with one word, "Whore" written on the case. At this point, Drake called Vespa, who called a detective friend. He was at GalUp within 30 minutes. Leo, the detective, asked the usual questions regarding evidence. Drake affirmed nothing had been touched except a corner of the package, thumb, and finger only.

"It's not leaving my sight." Drake stated.

Leo sized him up. "I'll get forensics to come here.

"Unmarked. I don't want any kind of publicity on this."

"Gotcha."

Vespa had arrived during this time and was pacing, talking, and texting. The men could tell she was PO'd and wisely kept silent. After forensics left, Vespa cut loose. If anyone had virgin ears, they didn't when she was done.

Leo spoke first. "I'll get the results asap, but I doubt anything will come of it. If it's who you say, record's probably squeaky clean."

"Leo," Vespa leaned over his chair, "somebody better find something. This is pure stalking, and we have evidence. Once we review what's on that," pointing to the disc, "we'll decide how to proceed."

"Sure Vespa." Leo stood, "You know I'll do it just for you."

Drake felt something between the two, smiled and kept silent. He booted his computer while Vespa walked Leo out. Upon her return, they sat in front of the computer as the disc loaded then played.

A mechanical voice spoke: "*You have gotten away with this immoral and disgusting behavior for too long. You lead men into the bowels of degradation, flaunting your whore body. This will stop you from destroying any more lives.*"

The picture switched to Cassie's face, the university photo Drake knew, and then to her performance from Friday night. The one that seduced the whole house at GalUp.

"How the hell did someone get in with a recording device? We have detectors." Drake growled.

"And it's a pretty darn good recorder too. Someone who was almost center stage." Vespa commented.

Drake grabbed his phone. "Security who worked Friday night." He spoke roughly. "Get them here now. And all discs from 6 p.m. to closing."

They watched the whole program, and the final picture was Cassie in her costume from Friday night, her face close up with the university photo next to it, leaving no doubt it was her.

The mechanical voice spoke again. "*This will be sent to all media outlets if something does not change. You have three weeks to correct the whore's behavior.*" Silence.

Drake went ballistic. Everything on his desk ended up on the floor, with Vespa managing to rescue the computer before it went as well. "I want these assholes brought down!" He shouted. "I will not be pressured or forced into this, and I will not allow Cassie to either. Not in any way."

"Settle down cowboy." Vespa soothed. "Let's see what Leo comes up with, then we'll start rocking worlds."

"Find out. And fast." He was still shouting. "I do not want Cassie to find out about this on the news." He had simmered to a growl.

Vespa smiled. "As least no one's figured out she's the major owner yet. That's when it really hits the fan."

Drake growled again, glaring mad. "Damn. I've got to interview girls now." Seeing the potential dancers file in. Turning to Vespa, "Find them. Today."

Vespa nodded then left with the disc in hand, just as determined as Drake, but keeping her temper temporarily in check. Drake went downstairs, joining Thomas to see what potential new talent GalUp might have. He knew a long weekend was in order. He settled in with Thomas and the auditions began.

CHAPTER 8

Sunday afternoon found Cassie excited about her potential find. A new star system that seemed similar to the one she lived in. The possibility that an alternate universe was in existence was back on the table.

She phoned Drake, left a message, and headed back to her ranch. With her head full of notes to be added to what she had, she almost missed her turn. Pulling in, Cassie noticed a van halfway up the drive. She stopped, dialed Drake, getting no answer, dialed the sheriff's office, then sat and waited.

The sheriff called back, telling her 15 minutes. Cassie dialed Drake again, not getting an answer, dialed Vespa. "Hey starlight! What's up?" Vespa answering her phone.

"Someone is at my ranch. I'm sitting here looking at the van."

"Do not confront them." Vespa warned. "Call the sheriff."

"Done. I don't see anyone moving around."

"Stay where you are. Drake just phoned and he's very close."

This caught Cassie off guard. "Why is he close and why did he call you?"

"Business, love. Nothing more." Vespa heard the accusing tone of Cassie's question.

About that time, Cassie saw a man and woman come from behind her house. The woman was snapping photos. They both paused upon seeing her car and hurried to the van. Cassie saw the sheriff's vehicle pull up behind her and breathed a sigh of relief. As he stepped up to Cassie's passenger side, the van rolled up. He directed them to stop. Cassie heard him order them out of the van. It was a news crew. Cassie drew in a sharp breath.

"These people don't belong here." Cassie yelled out the window. "Tell her to stop taking pictures. And I want the disc those photos are on."

The sheriff stepped over to the van. Cassie couldn't hear the conversation but saw the nods "no" and the hands making comments. As the sheriff turned back to Cassie's car, Drake pulled up behind her and was out in a flash, telling her to stay put.

She heard Drake tell the sheriff the same thing she had told him, holding his hand out. The lady became very animated, refusing to hand it over. The conversation became even more animated, and both refused to budge. Drake was on his phone and Cassie heard the words court order. The woman handed the camera to the sheriff, who then took the disc out, asked for all the other cameras as well, took those discs, and returned the cameras. After getting their credentials and leaving, both the sheriff and the news van, Drake motioned for Cassie to drive to the house, following her himself.

"What was that about?" Cassie questioned as they walked to the house.

"I guess about you." Drake replied. "We need to talk."

Sitting at the table, Drake filled Cassie in with what had transpired the day before. She sat in stunned silence, trying to assimilate and make sense of what had been told to her. Drake just sat watching the emotions cross her face, feeling strongly protective. "Obviously they lied to us."

"Ya think!?" Cassie looked up. "Tyler has screwed me once again."

"We don't think all of it's Tyler or his father. The newspaper, possibly. We're waiting on the editor as well as results from the disc."

"What do I do, Drake?" Cassie questioned. "All I've wanted to do is what I'm doing right now. I never asked for anything I didn't earn or work my ass off for."

"I know, babe." Drake took her hand. "It's the evil in the world that gangs up and tries to destroy the good."

"Wrong." Cassie made a buzzer sound. "It's the assholes with the money that think they own you."

"True, babe." Drake ran his hand down her arm and Cassie pulled away. "But we do our best to fight back and keep them from winning."

Drake's phone rang, causing Cassie to jump a little. "Yes, Vespa."

As Cassie listened and watched Drake, a sense of dread made her hands go cold and breath hitch. The frown on Drake's face made it worse.

"I'll tell her. See you tomorrow then." Drake said, laying his phone on the table. Cassie watched him expectantly. Drake took a deep breath before relaying what Vespa told him. He was trying to stay calm while wanting to destroy something.

"I don't know how that woman does it, but she can find anything. I need her trade secrets." Drake half-smiled.

"What is it, Drake?" Cassie asked, not smiling.

"The video isn't from Tyler or his father. That's the good news. The notes might be difficult to determine. Vespa said they found two distinct fingerprints, two on the disc case and one on the disc itself. One of the ones on the disc case belongs to a guy who makes videos. Not the type to be seen by the public. He's been ID'd several times, being connect to bootleg porn." Drake felt his temper rise again as he explained things to Cassie. "He said a suit brought a phone recording and pictures, giving instructions on what he wanted."

Cassie held her hand up. "Wait. We have a no camera rule. How?"

"Don't know yet but either one of the girls or cleaning staff left it for money. Everyone is screened before getting in."

"Well, looks like a good old Q&A is in order. Now what about the second print?" Cassie queried.

"Nothing yet. Vespa is going to pull her DMV strings and see what might pop up. That's all we have right now. All porno guy said was the guy was a suit. Didn't have anything else."

"Damn." Cassie shook her head. "Maybe someone else from the university wants me gone. This is unreal."

"You'll be safer in town. You can stay with me." Drake offered.

"Cassie smiled. "No. I won't run off scared" She stook and took a set of keys off a peg by the door. "You can lock the gate on your way out."

"Cass..."

"No, Drake." She held her hand up. "I still need time alone. I have a head full of notes, I would like a shower, and I need to prep for class tomorrow. If I'm still allowed on campus." She paused." Who all knows about the video?"

Drake stared at Cassie. "I don't think you need to be alone. Just follow me back. You can have the extra bedroom."

"Look, Drake," Cassie laid her hand across his arm, "I know we need to talk about the other night, but not on top of the mess going on right now. I just need my space tonight."

Drake resigned himself to Cassie's wishes. As he left, he phoned the sheriff's office and asked for someone to keep watch. They assured him they would. Tomorrow, whether Cassie liked it or not, a security gate was going up. He was tired and disgusted when he got home and ended up on the sofa with a glass of bourbon. Sleep came hours later.

Cassie locked all the doors and windows, then went to the kitchen to pour herself a drink. Bourbon on the rocks relaxed her as she headed to her study. She booted her computer, pulled her notes from her briefcase, and began dictating her weekend findings. She mused on the possibilities and noted to contact Rafe's and have them help her determine what she found.

"Hey star gazer." Her enchantress self spoke, startling her. "You let that hunky dude slip away. I was all ready for some action."

"Go away." Cassie growled. "I've more important things happening right now. This could save my career."

"You're still interested in that mess? At your age, settling down should be a priority." Enchantress Cassie sniggered.

"Look," Cassie was not in the mood for her enchantress. "I have to prove myself academically first. Yes, I am now probably out of time, but I know there's something out there and I believe I just found it. I've got two weeks to make things happen."

"You have an awesome life ahead of you, doll." Enchantress Cassie seemed eager to talk tonight. "You found what you need so prove and let's live a little. Hunky man won't wait forever."

"Drake," Cassie emphasized his name, "is free to do whatever he wishes." Then thought to herself, "Not true. I don't want to share him."

"Then don't!" Enchantress Cassie shouted, causing Cassie to jump to her feet.

Finishing her backup, Cassie stored it in her safe, closed her electronics down and decided to go to her perch at the barn, hoping her other self would go away. No such luck.

"Could you imagine the lovemaking up here!" Emitting a sexy growl. "Just you, him, and nature." Another sexy growl followed.

"Lay off." Cassie giggled, feeling a tingle of excitement. "I need to get through all of this mess first. Someone wants me out of both of my spaces now it seems." Sighing, she took another sip of her drink. "Thing is, only one person comes to mind, and I think his daddy is pushing him to do so. Unfortunately, I don't know why. I just told the boy no, kneed him, and left." Cassie sighed deeply.

"He's no boy. And self-righteous people want what they want no matter the cost, right? But you found your man, found your stars, now you have to make the dream come true." Enchantress Cassie nudged a naughty thought out causing Cassie to shiver.

"No! He knows something about the club he's not telling me."

"Then ask him, stupid."

"It's all piling up so fast. I need to concentrate on one thing at a time right now." Cassie puffed.

"Look girl," Enchantress Cassie puffed back, "life gets over busy sometimes. Deal. You've got to get him back over here. All of us only have a certain amount of time here to help you. Let's make the best of it."

"I don't have time for a relationship. I'm not ready. I just found this star system, something's wrong at GalUp, and I'm on borrowed time at the university." Cassie was getting frustrated. "I will get to everything, just not him right now. No."

"You need to decide your path. Hell, our path. You're one of the hottest 45-year-olds on the market. But you are 45. Life is changing. You shouldn't be living like a nun. At least enjoy your newfound sex life."

"I'm not a slut."

"Neither am I." Enchantress Cassie harrumphed.

"Doesn't sound that way."

"Shut up. You've never listened to your heart. But since the happy night, it's been drawn out. You've got a war going on, you just need to find a solution. Do you give in, give up, or figure out how to make peace?" Enchantress Cassie took a deep breath. "Look, I'm as smart as you, I mean, I am you, just the side that has more fun. Well, not right now. You contact who you need about the star system, aright. It's not like you can hop on a rocket and go check things out. Then mark it done, holding, and move on. Check one thing off your holy grail list and move to the next."

Cassie sighed, knowing her enchantress self was right. "Dang it! We need more advanced ways to confirm stuff. I hate waiting."

Enchantress Cassie sniggered. "I can think of a lot of fun things to do while waiting."

Exasperated, Cassie grumbled. "Just shut up. Everything isn't about sex."

"Not true. Let's look at the reporters. Why were they here? University, GalUp or both? Someone is out to get something. We're either the forefront or caught in the middle. Time for the thinking cap again. But," Enchantress Cassie paused dramatically, "before I go for now, you've got to think of our future. I feel love in the air. Don't let it pass by or murder it. Read the signs girl and take heed. Ta."

Cassie felt alone then. She stared up, just breathing, emptying her jumbled thoughts. She had never felt this scattered before and it was leaving a sour taste. "Prioritize." She spoke. "Go back to the lists." But for now, she was tired, mentally exhausted, and needed sleep. Shooting back her last sip of bourbon, she headed to the house and sleep, failing to notice the sheriff's cruiser at her front entry.

On her way out the next morning, Cassie saw the sheriff's cruiser. "Drake." She thought as she waved to the deputy. Her class was full as usual, and she was excited to share her findings. Lots of questions exploded as soon as her presentation was completed, as well as an email from NASA confirming her findings. This brought a hardy round of applause from her students.

After completing her classes, talking with an astronomer about how to handle the information, and being congratulated by the dean, Cassie felt as if she was personally flying in the stars. Sitting in her office, she prepared everything for her classes the next day, when the door opened and in strode Tyler and his father. She dialed 911 on her cell and kept her finger on the send button.

"You need to leave." Cassie stood. She was in fight or flight mode and did have sense enough to turn her desktop recorder on.

"No." Tyler said. "We're gonna talk. Your friggin' attorney won't give me the time of day and your bulldog just keeps threatening me. The university has warned me out of your space, so I had to take my own initiative to talk to you."

"Seems like there's reason, Tyler. You're trying to ruin my career here, all for a lousy grade and kick to the groin."

"Cassie," Tyler sat in the chair across from her, "I need the grades. I did wrong by you. Way wrong. I'm on academic probation because of it if that makes you feel any better. They believed you in your interview."

"Then why all the notes, Tyler? Or is that daddy's doing?" She pointed to Tyler's father. Both men looked surprised and then nodded negatively in an unspoken Q&A. Right then, Cassie felt a shot of fear snake up her spine. Tyler's surprised look threw Cassie off, but she didn't show that to them.

"Look." She showed the face of her phone. "I've got the police dialed up. If you don't leave, I'll have you both arrested. And since there's a restraining order, it won't be so easy to bail out."

Tyler moved to the door, as did his father, but neither man left. "Cassie, wait." Tyler motioned with hands, "We've come to apologize. Well, I've come to. I did make up the lies. I was scared, mad, and put out by your rejection."

"Really!?" Cassie snorted.

"I've managed to pass most of my classes. The ones I couldn't, I played or paid. It worked with everyone except you. When I eavesdropped on your conversation while in Tennessee, I thought I had the perfect plan to make you pass me." He lowered his head. "Obviously it didn't, and you don't know how sorry I really am."

Cassie sighed deeply but kept her guard up. "And my funding? You?" Pointing to Tyler's father.

The man nodded affirmatively and also hung his head.

Cassie snorted again. "And this has nothing to do with what I discovered? It's all coincidence?"

"You discovered something?" Tyler exclaimed questioningly. "Totally amazing. I'm truly excited for you."

"Then you don't know?"

"How could I? You banned me from your class, and no one will talk to me now. I'm in college hell."

At that moment, Cassie knew the truth, she believed what Tyler told her. Would it bite her in the butt? Probably. But Tyler did know her work and he was actually quite knowledgeable at what he knew. She decided to go with her gut and put her phone down. Motioning to the chairs, she told father and son to sit. She called Vespa and Drake, conferencing them in on the conversation. After explaining her belief about Tyler's lack of involvement in the letter campaign, she told Vespa to drop the restraining order.

"Tyler is on academic probation," she glared at him, "and I will hold that over his head at present. I am going to allow him back in class, if he wishes, and continue as my assistant, but only on campus. There will be a truckload of contingencies which I will note and send to Vespa for a contractual agreement. Is everyone okay with this?"

The two men in the room nodded, she heard frustrated yesses from Vespa and Drake. "Thank you. I'll call in a bit." Disconnected and squared up with Tyler.

"Thank you, Cassie." He spoke genuinely as far as she could tell.

Cassie threw daggers. "Don't thank me yet. You caused a lot of trouble. You bushwhacked me and tried to steal my work. That is inexcusable. You've got a long way to go to rebuild that trust. You also tried to disprove my work, saying you don't believe in what I'm looking for."

Tyler nodded, shifting in his chair, looking very guilty.

"That being said, Vespa will draw up a contract that you will sign if you want to come back as my assistant. Plain and simple, if you attempt any type of subterfuge or sabotage, you will be dismissed, thrown out of university, and jailed. No one but us will know of this and if it gets out, it's by you."

Tyler leaned forward, putting his hands on her desk. "Cassie, I won't screw you over. I really am interested in astrology. I do want to be as good as you someday. I'll happily sign and do as you request."

Tyler's father stood first and spoke sheepishly. "I also apologize, Dr. Hunter. Parents sometimes do wrong to help their children and I know I'm the worst offender. He is now on his own academically to pass or fail."

Cassie nodded, accepting the apology.

"We will take our leave. And I assure you, the note you mentioned did not come from us."

After they left, Cassie felt the tension leave her body. While not shaking, she felt like a bundle of nerves. She texted Vespa what she wanted in the contract. Texting Drake, she said she would see him Friday at GalUp. To both of them, she noted that the notes appeared to not have come from either Tyler, or his father and they were back to square one. The drive home relaxed her until she found a gate blocking her entrance. Immediately she dialed Drake.

"I know you're mad." Was how he answered the phone.

"What the hell!" Cassie yelled into the phone.

"Cassie, after the reporters, I thought it better to do this."

"Drake, I'm safe here. One way in, one way out. I'll see anyone driving up."

Drake tried to placate her. "Babe, I know you're perfectly safe there. This is so I won't worry. You know the code already."

Cassie punched in G-A-L-U-P, and the gate swung open and automatically closed behind her. She did feel safter, but Drake wasn't off the hook. "Next time you make changes, ask me first." She ordered.

"Yes, babe." He spoke softly. "Wish I could see you before tomorrow."

Cassie felt warmth flood her body at the husky sound of his voice, but she held steadfast in her needing to still be alone for the time being.

"I know, Drake. Just need to settle things first."

"One step at a time, right?" He asked.

"Goodnight."

"Sleep sweet, babe."

CHAPTER 9

Sleeping was again out of the question, so Cassie just sat on her porch watching the lights in the distance and the stars above. She wondered about her star system and what NASA researchers might find. Knowing it would take time, she contemplated the potential of life, if any, or even a parallel life to earth. She didn't doubt other life forms existed, she just wanted proof.

As she thought about her find, her mind also wandered to GalUp and what was happening there. Drake had mentioned a couple of meetings, but she couldn't recall whether he had told her about them or gave her a copy of the minutes. She noted to ask the next time she saw him. She still had a vision for the whole area and needed to find out what was happening with that last building.

Between all that was happening since Tennessee, she'd gotten off track of her life goals. She'd found the stars, not sure yet about the university or GalUp but moved those to the top of her get to the bottom of things list. Then Enchantress Cassie interrupted her thoughts.

"You forgot your man."

"Shut up."

"Nope." Enchantress Cassie laughed. "Nothing more important than your man."

"I'm trying to get things straightened out right now. I lost track, I... Wait. Why am I explaining this to you?

"Good question." Enchantress Cassie smirked mentally. "Why don't you call him over so you two can discuss, heavy on the discuss, work?

"You're so full of crap." Cassie snarked. "What do you want?"

"Well, I'm not here for our health. Could be soon, but that's for another day. I'm trying to get your seductress to kick in a bit. Now that you've had a taste, I'm surprised you don't want more." Cassie heard a breathy sigh. "We are in our 40s, sexless, and could be manless soon. You've finally broke the bed, so to speak, but no follow-up. Now you're saying you've got to get things in order?"

Cassie knew her other self was right, but she couldn't let go of the nagging feeling she was missing something. Something vital that would affect the rest of her life. She just couldn't put her finger or her mind on it.

Enchantress Cassie sounded exasperated when she spoke. "Just make your stupid list and get on with things. We don't like surprises, but I have a feeling there's gonna be a few to put up with here pretty soon."

"Don't speak them in, please." Cassie almost begged. "I'm leaning on the side of aggravated and frustrated, borderline panicked. Everything is up in the air with no sign of landing soon."

"So, make something happen. Two things. Week three for the university is at an end, one to go. Instead of farting around town, go to your place. Stick your nose in things. Tomorrow night, blast down the walls."

"You're probably right." Cassie sighed deeply. "Nervous energy makes for good dancing."

"Now you're talking. And find out what the heck is going on with all these meetings." Enchantress Cassie nudged with determination.

Cassie nodded.

Enchantress Cassie gave an almost lewd laugh. "Who knows, you might get a bang out of the manager too."

"Slut. So not nice."

"Prude." And Cassie felt alone again.

She started working on her newest mental list, trying to get her mind wrapped around the busyness. She felt herself doze off and stretched on the sofa, instantly asleep, only to wake five hours later to her phone buzzing.

Vespa sounded excited. "Well, we always like early wakeup calls, right? I waited as long as I could stand. 6:00 a.m. is a good time to start the day."

"Vespa," Cassie sleepily murmured, "I've got class at 8:30, thanks for the call. News?"

"Darlin'" she spoke her best Texan/Italian voice." The university dropped all the charges, so to speak. Your tenure is safe. Classes stay as is. Only no grant money." She must have forgotten about the new grantor.

"Wow!"

"Yeah, wow!" Vespa laughed. "Their attorney said it had all be a huge mistake. They could find no wrongdoing."

Cassie knew why or thought she did and remined Vespa about the previous day. Vespa almost shouted. "You really think that man has that kind of pull? And you're willing to trust that little turd?"

"Oh, no. Not one ounce of trust." She mentioned about the reason for the contract." It's going to be total lockdown for a while, but I am willing to forgive."

"Nicer than me." Vespa snarled. "I'll have it ready before you head to GalUp today. In fact, I'll just leave it there for you."

"For my eyes only, please."

"Done."

Dashing out the door, she had the drive and possibly 20 minutes to spare before her class. Entering the theater that day, she gave directions to Tyler, set up her slide show, and class was over before she knew it. As she headed through Dallas, she noted how beautiful daylight was. It had been so long since she noticed it. She noted to herself to take some weekends just to relax. Cassie arrived at GalUp around noon. She did a drive around her block looking at the booming businesses, glad to have purchased it all. Upscale but not snooty.

As she pulled into GalUp's parking area, she took note of the extra cars. "Maybe a staff meeting." She thought. She wasn't quiet about entering through the back and didn't see anyone but security who nodded with a smile and motioned her in. As she started for the elevator, she heard voices in the conference room and headed in that direction. It sounded a little heated as she stopped just outside the door.

"If we don't draw the regular wage earners, they'll start making noise that this part of Dallas is too rich." It was a twangy male voice speaking.

"And if the university presses their issue, people will flock here and claim the same thing when they can't afford the door cover charge." A second deeper male voice spoke.

She heard an exasperated female voice speak next. "Look Drake, we get that this is an upscale area, but if we have another similar lower scale place, put a café in the space above it, we can draw in regular class people, and they might even try to save for a high-class night at GalUp."

Drake sounded tired and agitated. "No. A strip joint is a strip joint, no matter how you try to class it up. Undesirables will show up and it will be a constant headache. Cassie will not allow it, and neither will I."

The female voice spoke, "Drake, it doesn't really matter now does it? We have the deciding vote. However it was managed, we have one more share than you two."

"Don't be too sure about things. How it was managed, I haven't figured it out yet, but I will. No strip joint. And if Cassie finds out, hell won't hide any of us."

The female spoke once more, and Cassie not only felt her blood rise but her heart drop. "It's too late now. Majority will be going into contract with a group who will have a gentleman's club open in three months with a mid-class restaurant above it."

Cassie heard Drake sigh. "I'll stop this."

"And Lady Cassandra," the woman snarked, "will finally have some competition. Maybe it's time to retire her." Long pause and Cassie felt ready to explode. "She's getting up in age. Plus, if people connect her to the university, it will put a bad light on both careers." Drake cleared his throat to speak but the woman continued. "What do you think would happen if everyone found out she was the owner? Do you want to see both careers crash as well as this company?" She sounded almost gleeful. "Get rid of her or we will."

Cassie had met the lady once she knew of but could not recall her name. Vespa came to mind to call about this woman as she listened to the remainder of the conversation. She heard a chair screech and Drake spoke in a low, deadly voice.

"Today is over for now. If I see any of you near Cassie, there will be no place you can hide. News gets out, even worse. She owns the buildings, not you. You have working capital shares in the corporation only. Don't go any further than that. I will correct this, with or without you. Don't fight me, you will lose."

"Drake," the female tried to sultry with her voice, "when you get over your little crush, you'll see that we are right. When she gets boring, come see me. I'll take care of you."

Cassie boiled as she bolted toward the stairs, texting Vespa as she did. She did not hear Drake's response to the woman.

"Lady, I'll moved to a monastery or castrate myself before I come to you." And stormed out of the room, leaving the men laughing and the woman seething.

Cassie stopped outside the office, knowing Drake would be there soon and knowing she had to play things cool. She saw the package Vespa promised in her box, grabbed it, and went to her desk.

As Drake barreled in, she pretended to be startled and put her finger on the contract as if she didn't want to lose her place. "Goodness. You look pissed."

"Yeah. Rough morning." He growled.

"Anything I can help with?" she asked.

"Not really." He didn't look at Cassie. "Just some legal crap that's not right."

"With GalUp?" She questioned.

Cassie saw him take a deep breath before he turned to face her. "Nothing major." She saw him grimace. "Something on a contract not worded right. I'll get it taken care of."

"I have time today. Maybe an extra pair of eyes will help." Cassie offered, trying to get Drake to open up and tell her what she had just found out.

"No." He shook his head. "Easy enough to fix. I just gotta run to the attorney and accountant."

"Liar!" She wanted to scream but instead spoke, "Drake, what's going on? You're really peeved, so I know it's something more."

Drake looked as if he wanted to spill everything. She watched as he physically and mentally pulled away. Grabbing his coat and briefcase, he headed out the door. "Tired I guess. Nothing I can't handle, babe. See ya later tonight." And was gone.

Cassie seethed. She wondered what else Drake was hiding. She found her financial statements, which she had read, but no notes about what was happening with the shareholders. Cassie knew a confrontation was coming and knew she had to be prepared, so she spent the rest of her time reviewing emails and financials, trying to find anything about what she heard. Nothing. She made a list of questions, with notes, to put to Drake.

If she heard right, a topless bar would be going into the last vacant building on the block. This, she would not allow. Going through some business connections, she scheduled an appointment for the following

Monday afternoon to discuss a business she had in mind. If Drake could keep secrets, she could as well.

Not wanting to stick around and eventually explode, Cassie took a walk around the properties she owned, visiting with the owners or managers, asking how they liked the area and what potential new businesses they thought might enhance it more. While she received a lot of ideas, nothing seemed to fit that particular spot. She stood in front of it and tried to picture many of the ideas, but still nothing so she headed back to her car and then home.

The rest of the week seemed oddly boring. Little to no contact from Drake or Vespa, just short texts about what was happening with the note hunting and how the university had backed completely down with their charges. So, she focused on her star system and communications with NASA, with promises of confirmation soon. By Friday, she was a nervous wreck, a little angry, and ready to blow off some steam.

In her office Friday night, Cassie noticed GalUp shareholders had booked a large party booth. Drake had not mentioned this or didn't know. Lady Cassandra would show them just how "old" she was. Sending her playlist to Thomas, she went to her dressing room to prepare. By the time her set was up, Cassie was pissed all over again and knew that Drake would get the hint by the music she had chosen. Old and new, but powerful songs. Tonight was her power play. Time to settle some shit.

She stayed in her dressing area, ignoring Drake as he completed his work. She caught him staring several times and wondered if he'd gut up and tell her what was going on, but nothing. "Time to take control." She told herself as her time slot came up. The light show was as powerful as her "chick songs" and the crowed was once again stunned into silence. Cassie had ordered all stages empty as she wanted all eyes center stage.

The stage was cloaked in darkness, a heavy silence filling on the room. The air was thick with anticipation. A single, blood-red spotlight pierced the darkness, illuminating Cassie as she stood center stage. Her head was bowed, her fists clenched at her sides. The faint sound of a heartbeat thundered through the speakers, slow and ominous, growing louder with each pulse.

Cassie was not just a dancer tonight, she was a warrior. The demons of the day clung to her like shadows, whispering doubts, hurling accusations, but she was ready. This stage was her battleground, and she would fight with every ounce of strength and defiance she possessed.

Cassie was dressed for war. She wore a black leather bodysuit, fitted like a second skin, with jagged red accents resembling the marks of battle. The bodysuit was sleeveless, showcasing her toned arms and the crimson-painted scars that snaked up her biceps. Across her chest was a harness of silver chains, clinking softly with every breath she took.

Her legs were clad in thigh-high boots with steel-toed tips, adding weight and impact to every step. Around her waist flowed a tattered, dark crimson sash, like a warrior's banner trailing behind her. Her hair was braided tightly, a warrior's crown, with strands of red woven through. Her eyes were lined heavily, fierce and unyielding, and her lips were painted a deep, defiant black.

The music began with a low, guttural chant, primal and ancient, as if calling forth the spirits of warriors long past. A haunting cello joined, its mournful wail underscoring the gravity of the battle ahead. Then, without warning, the music shifted, a thunderous drumbeat crashed through the silence, accompanied by sharp, staccato strings. The sound was electric, a battle cry in musical form. The crowd gasped.

Cassie's head snapped up with the first drumbeat, her eyes blazed with unyielding fire. She stepped forward, her movements sharp and deliberate, each step a challenge to the demons that have haunted her. She struck her chest with her fist, a defiant thud echoing through the room. Her body began to move in time with the relentless rhythm, powerful, aggressive, unstoppable.

Cassie marched across the stage, her boots slamming down in time with the pounding drums. Each stomp sent a shockwave of energy through the floor, as if she was shattering the ground beneath her.

She threw her arms out in a sweeping motion, slicing through the air as though cutting down invisible enemies. Her hands clenched into fists, and she spun rapidly, her sash whipping around her like a crimson blur.

Cassie crouched low, her arms raised as if shielding herself from an onslaught. Then, in a sudden burst of energy, she sprung forward, delivering a powerful kick that reverberated through the stage, her body a weapon of strength.

As the music intensified, Cassie's movements became more frantic, more desperate. She punched the air, her fists colliding with invisible barriers. She leapt and landed with a force that shook the stage, her arms outstretched, daring the world to knock her down. Her body twisted and turned, each motion a battle, each breath a story of her strength.

The stage lighting shifted, casting jagged shadows that seem to move and writhe around her. These shadows represented the demons, the voices of doubt, fear, and those who sought to destroy her spirit. They closed in, circling her as the music built to a chaotic crescendo.

Cassie faltered, dropping to one knee as if the weight of the day had finally brought her down. Her head bowed once more, and for a brief moment, the audience wondered if she has been defeated or hurt.

But then, the cello's mournful wail shifted into a triumphant melody, supported by the steady rise of drums. The chant returned, louder and more powerful, no longer a dirge but a victory cry. Cassie lifted her head, her eyes blazing with determination.

She rose slowly, deliberately, every muscle in her body coiled with strength. Her movements became fluid yet fierce, a combination of raw power and grace. She spun, leapt, and struck with renewed energy, her fists and kicks landing with thunderous precision.

Cassie threw her head back and let out a silent scream, her mouth open wide, her body vibrating with the force of her defiance. The audience could feel it, the unspoken roar of a woman who refused to be broken.

She charged toward the edge of the stage, slamming her fists into the ground and rising with a fierce kick that seemed to send the shadows scattering. She turned, driving her arms through the air as though throwing the weight of her past off her shoulders.

The music reached its final, climactic peak, a fusion of triumphant strings and pounding drums that echoed like the heartbeat of a victorious warrior. Cassie moved to the center of the stage, her body a blur of motion as she delivered her final, powerful strikes. With a final leap, she landed in a wide stance, her arms raised high above her head, her fists clenched in triumph.

The lights dimmed, leaving only the red spotlight that bathed her in a victorious glow. The music faded into a soft, peaceful hum, and Cassie slowly lowered her arms, placing a hand over her heart. Her chest rose and fell with deep, calming breaths.

As the audience watched, Cassie closed her eyes, her face softening. A quiet, serene smile spread across her lips. She has fought her demons, faced the darkness, and emerged stronger. In this moment, she is at peace.

Every moment of this dance has been a release, a catharsis. Cassie felt the fire of her anger, her pain, and her defiance burn away the weight of her day. She knew she had won, not just against the external forces that sought to bring her down, but against the internal doubts that threatened to consume her.

As she stood on the stage, victorious and unbroken, Cassie felt the quiet strength of her soul. She was a warrior, a survivor, and she knew now that no matter what challenges came her way, she would rise to meet them. She has fought the battle within and emerged victorious, and the peace that follows was hers to keep. This is her truth, her power, her victory. She is unstoppable.

Cassie knew what her immediate future held. She looked at the mirror above the crowd where she knew Drake was watching and then left the stage.

Not bothering to change, Cassie grabbed the stuff she had left by the back door and left the building. At the ranch, she showered and went to the barn. No lights, no star gazing, just breathing. Drake had texted several times, she didn't read them, just shut her phone off. She then changed the code to the entry gate, went to her office and began prep for Monday. She began ticking things off her list. Confronting Drake was left for Monday afternoon, late. She'd corner him at the club. After popping out all her emails, setting her schedule, she rescheduled with the businesspeople from Monday to Sunday in Fort Worth.

To her surprise, sleep came quickly. No interruptions. At 10 a.m. she woke, feeling completely refreshed and still empowered. Cassie called as well as emailed NASA about her star system. While she had acknowledgment about it being uncharted, she had no confirmation of her being the discoverer. That was what she needed most. Cassie gave herself the rest of the morning to do whatever struck her fancy. She ignored her phone and emails, choosing to look for potential businesses for the empty building. Something classy but not expensive. Able to meet the needs of regular income people. Then it hit her.

Her business ventures included almost anything people wanted, but no comedy club. Something for up-and-coming comedians and a dinner theater above. After looking up clubs in the area, she found only one dinner comedy club, and that was in Fort Worth. She would visit it before her meeting that night. Cassie gathered her proposal and headed to Fort Worth. She enjoyed the show, talked with the owner about a potential one opening elsewhere, and found him to be quite amiable about it. After that, she knew that the circle had been completed with her buildings and headed to an office supply outlet to get the proposal typed out and printed for the meeting later.

The meeting went as expected, perfect. Most people in the business world of Texas wanted to invest in Cassie's enterprises, Jake Calhoun was no exception. He and his wife loved GalUp, had missed the investment opportunity, but jumped on this one, including the dinner theater above the club.

That night, Cassie texted out that the next shareholder meeting be rescheduled to Thursday to fit her class schedule. After several back-and-forth emails, it was accomplished. She was feeling good, but the next email threw a kink in the whole works.

An email from the woman shareholder showing the stock buy that took away Cassie's controlling interest in GalUp. She had heard this that fateful day in GalUp but didn't believe it. Now with proof, the battle had become very personal. She knew she personally owned the land and buildings, but really wanted to know how she lost controlling interest in GalUp Corp. A quick email to Vespa to find this out and report only to her. If Drake had been turned somehow, this battle had now become hers alone and was one she was not willing to lose.

CHAPTER 10

Monday found her at the university early, waiting for Tyler to show up. She opened her office door to find an envelope on the floor. Carefully opening it, Cassie found another note, which she snapped a photo of and sent to Vespa, telling her she would drop the original off later.

Tyler showed up on time and in her exasperation, Cassie laid down the law again. "I will not tolerate anything but cooperation, Tyler. My research, my studies, anything to do with my work stays in this office. You will be the first person that gets questioned should anyone find out about the extra theories or my outside life. You will be under probation until I deem a time you're not. Is this all clear? Do you have any questions?"

Tyler agreed with everything, asked no questions, and signed the contract without hesitation. He thanked Cassie again and promised to help in any way possible. He told her he was very happy about her findings and was ready to research it for her.

Cassie thanked him, told him she'd get a copy of the contract to him, and set him to researching a smaller set of stars around the one she'd discovered, reminding him to take meticulous notes. After class was done and all paperwork noted and tucked away in her safe, Cassie set a trip to Rafes for her, Tyler and three other students in a week to assess all the info collected and mark coordinates then headed to Vespa's.

Vespa was fit to be tied, which she never was. "I can't find a link to all of this. I was sure it was the kid or his dad. Even more so, someone from the university, but nothing."

"The newspaper article?" Cassie asked.

"Nothing."

"What about the notes?"

"Same. Nothing on the extra fingerprints either. Whoever it is has no record."

"Damn!" Cassie threw her hands up. "What have I done that's so wrong?"

"Not a thing. Someone is out for blood, yours, and is good at hiding. Now we have to uncover them." Vespa shook her head. "We need them to make a mistake."

"Yeah. But how since we don't know who to go after."

Vespa nodded deeply and agreed. They finished their business and Cassie headed off to GalUp. Not her normal routine, but she decided it was time to start making her presence known again. Since her university schedule had changed, she would make adjustments to be at GalUp a little more often. The guard was surprised. Cassie just nodded and entered as he opened the door. Hearing nothing downstairs, she headed up to her and Drake's office, pausing when she heard him speaking.

"She's gonna fight it and you know it." He spoke harshly. Then listened to the person on the other end. "She doesn't have a choice. It will be voted on Thursday. You don't have enough votes to stop it."

Cassie figured it was that woman from the shareholder's meeting. Dang, if she could just remember her name. She swung the door open. Drake looked shocked.

He spoke. "Cassie." Then to the phone. "We'll talk later."

Cassie quickly spoke. "Don't let me interrupt. Go right ahead with your conversation. I have some free time so thought I'd get caught up here."

Drake disconnected. "What's up, babe?" he stood coming around the desk.

Cassie quickly went to her desk. "I've got to catch up on my paperwork before Thursday."

"Thought you had everything at home. Wasn't expecting you until then." He smiled as he walked over. "I could have brought copies and gone through them with you."

While the comment did send a tingle through Cassie, she was still mad and suspicious, especially after him just disconnecting his phone call so quickly. "It's all good." She turned away from Drake. "I need to get back to being more involved anyway. Things just don't feel right so thought I'd stick my nose back in a bit." She turned to face Drake who had stopped beside her desk, his face set in stone. "What's new that I need to know about?"

Drake knew that was a question as loaded as the music she danced to the past Friday night. His next move would decide the course of the day, hell, even the week and it was not something he was looking forward to. He knew he needed to be open and honest, he was just still in shock that something like this had got away from him. Embarrassment played a key role as well. He was supposed to be taking care of their business and now the money grabbers had taken control. Since he hadn't figured out how yet, he didn't want to seem the failure he felt like.

Cassie was looking at him expectantly. Somewhere inside he knew she knew. Now he had to either stay his course of keeping it quiet or tell her she was no longer majority stockholder. With a sigh, Drake motioned to the sofa area. Cassie went to one of the chairs, she wasn't in any mood to sit close to Drake at that moment. He sighed deeply again and sat across from her.

Drake saw the anger in Cassie's eyes but couldn't bring himself to speak just yet, so Cassie helped him out. "I got an interesting email yesterday. I bet you can even guess what it's about." Cassie glared at Drake.

Drake lowered his head, then slowly raised back up to meet Cassie's glare. "Honestly, I was hoping for a little more time to figure out how it all happened."

Cassie snorted.

"Look," Drake reached out, but Cassie ignored his hand, "this should never have happened. It did. I didn't see or catch it. They pounced fast. Hanna Corbitt," recognition hit Cassie, "came to me the day they became majority shareholders two months ago." And Drake told her everything. This happened before she went to Tennessee, before the Tyler crisis, and he still never shared it with her. That's what hurt the most. Drake finished. "I didn't tell you because I thought I could fix it. Buy the shares back for you. They won't do it."

"So, we just let them destroy what we've built? They have control over all the businesses we own, Drake, right? We didn't break down each into its own corporation, we just put it all under GalUp."

Drake nodded. "We did, never dreaming this would happen."

"And they want a strip club."

"Yes."

"What else, Drake?" Cassie knew most of what he told her, but her gut was telling her there was more. "What else?" She repeated.

Drake walked to his desk, pulled a document from the drawer, and returned to Cassie. "This was delivered yesterday."

Cassie read through the papers, the feeling of dread causing a flush to run through her. "Can they do this? Can they force me out of a business I founded?"

"You can be fired, yes." Drake held up a hand. "But they must prove incompetence or harm to the business to remove you from the board. You have done neither so you should be safe."

Cassie's glare became even harder towards Drake. "Am I? What about the things going on at the university?"

"I thought that was all settled."

"Yeah. Except for the notes, Drake. I took the latest to Vespa this morning after class. Someone is trying to ruin both careers and I have no idea why."

"Babe," Drake sounded tired and exasperated, "I'm trying to find out as well. I've questioned everyone I know. Nothing. You're respected and loved at both places. Whoever it is, they are very good at hiding."

Cassie just sat in silence, knowing she had no time to make everything work. She was fighting everyone it felt like. She was tired. She knew her next moves would decide her future. Resolve steeled in her stomach. The battle lines were drawn, now how to fight back was the question. She heard her phone. It was Tyler. He said he needed to speak to her privately. It was very important. She offered to meet him, he told her he was outside the club. She buzzed security who brought him straight to the office.

Tyler started when Drake stood up. "Tyler."

"Sir."

"Were you following Cassie? Is that how you knew she was here?" Drake questioned.

"No, sir. She wasn't on campus, and I thought someone here might be able to reach her."

"She's right here if you care to talk to her." Cassie broke in. "Is this something that couldn't wait until tomorrow?"

Tyler looked at Drake, then back to Cassie.

"It's okay. He'll hear about it anyway so take a seat." Cassie motioned to the sofa.

"I was working late on one of our, uh, your projects and heard a noise, unusual noise out in the hall. Like tearing." He paused, trying to stay collected under Drake's stare. "I walked out and saw a lady tack something on your door then walk away really fast. She was smartly dressed like a lawyer, so I figured she was from the adjuncts office and went back to finish up. When I left, I saw this." Tyler handed a scrap of paper to Cassie. "It is a nasty note." Cassie handed it off to Drake.

Tyler looked very nervous. "Cassie, I only touched one corner. I didn't want anyone to see it, especially since I was the only working late. And after all…" He let the sentence trail. Cassie felt suspicion rise but decided to trust Tyler at this point. They had just settled things.

Drake stood. "Could you identify this woman if you were shown a photo?"

"Pretty sure I could. The video was still on in the hall too. If we call right now, they won't delete anything." Tyler volunteered.

Drake stepped away and began making phone calls. Cassie kept eye contact with Tyler, who seemed to have calmed a bit. She saw him take a deep breath. "Look Cassie, I promise it wasn't me. I'm not gonna screw our truce up. And I was thinking about the newspaper article too. Could it be the same person?"

Drake spoke first. "Possible. I'll check with them as well. The university will have the footage ready Wednesday. I'll send a photo of a possibility with Cassie when you go to view the footage. One day should be okay."

Cassie was getting very nervous. She could feel herself flushing hot and needed a release. To Tyler she spoke. "I'll see you in the morning then. Life as normal. Don't say a word to anyone. If you see that woman, contact campus security and have her held."

Tyler shook his head affirmatively. "Yes, ma'am. I'll try to snap a photo as well."

"Just don't spook her. We need to identify her first." Cassie stood and extended her hand. "Thank you, Tyler."

"Thank you, Cassie." He replied. "And I promise, I won't let you down."

Cassie needed out so she grabbed her things, but Drake stopped her. "Cass, we need to talk. About a lot of things."

Cassie breathed deeply. "I know we do, Drake. I know. But not until after Thursday. I'll be at the shareholder's meeting. I've got an idea to present. No, I'm not telling anyone until I have it finalized."

"It better be good. These guys are out for blood." He paused and let her arm go. "I never meant for this to happen. No matter what it looks like. I hope you believe that." His eyes glistened with unshed tears as he turned away from her.

"I'm trying to believe you, Drake." She placed her hand on his back. "There's just so much going on and it's hitting all at once. Dinner, Saturday." Then left GalUp.

Her email to the Calhoun's had come back with the amount they wanted to invest as well as a game plan for reconstruction of the two floors. Cassie was impressed, excited, and felt liberated. She scheduled a date with them and Vesta for the following week. All this mess would hopefully be over by then. She'd made it through the past few weeks with the university and the end of her four weeks was just days away.

The Calhoun's had solved one problem, and she emailed Vespa to send them a letter of good faith and intent for the two bottom floors. She showered and walked out to her loft above the barn, tried searching the stars, but tonight, they held no interest for her. She hadn't received anything from NASA and was just tired enough for her heart not to be in the right place.

"Hello, young lady." A soft motherly voice spoke. It was a voice of wisdom and calmed her completely.

"Hello." Cassie responded. "Which one are you?"

The gentle voice laughed. "One that shouldn't be here, and yet, here I am. Go inside, please."

Cassie went to her room and the chair beside the mirror. What she saw startled her a little bit. A much older version of herself but every bit as beautiful as she was now.

"What do you think?" The older version of herself asked.

Cassie laughed. "Beautiful."

"Now you know that about your future self. I am the Mother Cassie." She informed Cassie.

"Just wow. And I'm guessing I get to grow old?" Cassie probed.

"Very old." Came the reply.

"Good. Can I ask some questions?"

"Of course."

"Did I find a parallel world and that's why you are appearing?"

There was a long pause before Mother Cassie answered. "That is not for me to know how to answer. The universe's future is beyond my scope of knowledge. I can say this, you did find something amazing and wonderful."

"That's good to know." Cassie smiled. "At least I can act crazy for a reason."

"You're not crazy. Never have been, never will be. It'll be a few years, but your find will set new standards for the known universe." Mother Cassie's reply excited Cassie.

"What about me and Drake? Is he my helpmeet? Will we have a life together, children?"

"So many questions. Let life take its course. If we know our future, we could screw things up." Mother Cassie laughed like someone being bombarded by childlike questions.

"Okay. I get that. Then tell me why I am having visions of my different selves? You are the third different one I've met."

"Well girl," Mother Cassie began, "when a soul is born, there are many parts that must come together to be one and complete. Depending on how a person grows in their life and the many that have found their true selves, is how many are born to their world each time. It could be 200, it could be 2. Only the Divine Creator knows, and He will help those who ask to find their whole soul."

Cassie looked at her mother self somewhat confused. Some of what she said made sense, but the many selves thing was still a bit confusing. "How, if we're in different worlds, can we find each other?"

"The whole universe is connected, girl." Mother Cassie continued. "It's not our physical selves that are connected, young one, it's our spiritual selves. The us we are trying to become. There are teachers, mothers, dancers, lovers. You get the picture. As a teacher searching, when both of you find the same connection and completion of what you're searching for, you become one and that door closes. As each part connects and completes, the true self finds wholeness. Now, if the uncomplete self reaches the end of their life, all the living other selves do also, and the cycle begins again for the ones that did not complete their journey."

"That seems kind of cruel." Cassie spoke softly.

Mother Cassie nodded. "But how cruel is it to know that a soul is not complete because of something it needs to settle? What if there is another being that soul needs to touch, teach, or love, and that will save a life? What if it is another child that is waiting to be brought into this world to complete its true self by touching that soul? Would you classify that as cruel?"

Cassie could only nod.

"So, you see, although we are basically here to complete ourselves, we are also here to help others accomplish their life goals as well. The circle repeats for many often." Mother Cassie paused to wipe a tear as Cassie did the same. "And with all that being said, my younger self, I hope to meet you someday down this road you are traveling now instead of having to start the journey again. I have shared too much as it is, but you have figured out more than most ever will in 20 lifetimes. Until we meet again." And Cassie just saw her own self in the mirror.

She didn't know how long she sat there with her head resting on the chair's back and eyes closed before she heard her voice again. Still soft but not as old.

"Not quite time for sleep yet, my love." Cassie looked in the mirror but only saw herself.

"Afraid to show yourself?" Cassie asked.

"I am showing myself." The new Cassie replied.

"But you look like me." Cassie looked harder to find a difference.

"Technically, we're all you, just different stages of your life." Was the comment. "I am your life now. I'm also known as the Sage."

Cassie stared and snorted. "Great. Another me trying to give me orders."

Sage Cassie laughed deeply, and the sound was rich, which caused Cassie to laugh as well. Sage Cassie was so quiet and still for a few minutes that Cassie thought she had left. She started to rise for bed. "I wasn't gone, just contemplating."

"About?" Cassie queried.

Sage Cassie smiled before her look turned serious. "You have so much happening right now, I hate to add to the list."

"Oh joy." Cassie remarked sarcastically. "I need to heap more on my plate right now."

Sage Cassie grimaced, and Cassie felt it. She knew this was probably something life changing. "Look at me." Sage Cassie directed. "You only see my face. Life has a way of throwing surprises when we least expect it. You can't tell me our Creator doesn't have a sense of humor."

"Oh geez." Cassie thought.

"Definitely. Oh geez will be spoke a lot very soon." Sage Cassie laughed. "You forget, we are the same person."

"Yeah, well..." Cassie murmured.

Sage Cassie smiled as one would smile at a child. "It's time for rest now. You're going to need it. Just remember this, those you think are the enemy are not. You are going to need their support in the next few days. You've got several huge changes that will test you, but you're strong enough to see them to the end. We'll talk more soon."

"Wait!" Cassie called as she watched the mirror image shift. "That info was so vague, I probably dreamt it."

"You'll know very soon that this wasn't a dream. Sleep sweet."

Cassie blew out a puff of air and crawled into bed. Tuesday had technically started, but she hoped to sneak in a couple of hours of sleep before the day officially started. Sleep came fast.

CHAPTER 11

Tuesday morning found Cassie with her head hung over the toilet, feeling like her guts were trying to come out. She finally stopped heaving 20 minutes later and cleaned herself up. Hot ginger tea eased her stomach as she prepared for her day.

Slowing as she neared her office, Cassie saw Tyler waiting outside her door. "Well," She queried, "anything new this morning?"

Tyler nodded negatively. "But I did get security to let us review earlier than tomorrow, but I'm afraid it's right now."

"I have class in 15 minutes." She exclaimed.

"I'll take your class if you'll allow and if you make it back, great, we'll take things from there. I'm texting them now to let them know. Go." He sent an uneasy Cassie away.

Cassie arrived at the security office and was immediately shown footage of her area from the previous Friday. She noted two people, one male, came during her class and looked like he was putting something on her door, but it was difficult to really tell because of all the foot traffic. Then nothing until late afternoon when she saw a woman paste something on her door and turn directly towards the camera. Cassie immediately texted Vespa, then told security to make a copy, and that a subpoena would be delivered soon. She watched up to the point Tyler came out of her office, saw the note, and ran out of the building. Security handed her a drive with the video, and she returned to her classroom.

Finishing her second and final class for the day, Cassie thanked Tyler again, leaving no explanation on things, and headed to Vespa's law firm. There, Vespa watched and ended up throwing a very vocal temper fit. Cassie just watched until Vespa finished. Vespa phoned Drake and told him to call the shareholder meeting for the next day, Wednesday and leave no room for backing out. Cassie changed her schedule as well, hoping all the crap going on was nearing an end. Cassie's stomach clenched. Racing to the bathroom followed by Vespa, Cassie retched into the commode.

"Cass." Vespa sounded concerned. "It's not going to be that bad. Just confrontation and empty threats."

"Hmph." Cassie gagged out. "Happened this morning too. Guess nerves on what the day might bring. I've never been sick like this before."

Vespa handed her a hand towel. "Well, nerves can do it. Better?"

Cassie stepped out, thanking Vespa. They went over some things dealing with the potential Calhoun deal, finishing with the meeting at GalUp tomorrow. Cassie stopped in GalUp but not finding Drake, grabbed her weekly paperwork and headed home. Drake phoned as she turned into her drive.

"Vespa told me you were sick." Was the first thing he said. "You okay? Should I come over?"

"Cassie sighed, still not ready to deal with Drake. "I'm okay. And no, don't come over. I'll see you tomorrow."

"Cass, babe," Drake sounded tired. "We need to talk." He paused. "About a lot of things."

"You've said that before." It just popped out of her mouth.

"And we keep getting interrupted." He popped back.

"Yeah, well..." Cassie left the sentence hanging, hoping for a scrap of something.

Drake sighed tiredly again. "Babe, I know there's a trust issue happening right now, but believe me, I'm on your side."

Cassie sighed as well. "Look, after tomorrow, we'll talk. I'm settling all this mess this week. Period. I've got things happening with the university and NASA and since the other is settled at present with them, I'm hoping after Sunday no more worries. Figure out how to fix the other, Drake. GalUp is mine." Cassie disconnected from the call.

Feeling very tired, Cassie stepped into the kitchen to fix a bite but found the thought of food disgusting so went to her room to rest. She would look over everything later.

"Hey there." She heard Sage Cassie and turned the mirror to the chair. "You look very tired."

"Is that the word for sick, disgusted, and angry?" Cassie growled out.

Sage Cassie snorted. "Girl, you just don't know yet. You'll be okay. Just have to get to the weekend."

"Thrill a minute. You're obviously here for a reason. What?"

"Just to support you, darling. You've got five days of what will seem hellish, but you'll do fine." Sage Cassie spoke soothingly, and Cassie felt it calming her.

"So GalUp will be mine again. Whew." Cassie felt relief.

"It will eventually. You'll have a lot of other things on your plate as well so don't get hung up on just one. Life has a funny way of making priorities change."

"Do what? I'm just getting to the point of getting all this past month straightened out and you're telling me there's more." Cassie's head dropped to her chest.

"Breathe."

"No."

"Breathe."

Cassie took a deep breath, felt her stomach turn, and flew to the bathroom. Standing at the sink a few minutes later, Sage Cassie was smiling back at her.

"Oh great!" Cassie threw her hands up in despair. "I get fat too?" Seeing the whole of Sage Cassie.

"In a sense." Sage Cassie touched her stomach, smiling.

It took a moment for what Cassie was seeing to register. Tears formed and she flew back to the toilet. Once back at the mirror, Sage Cassie's face was all that could be seen.

Cassie was crying. "No. Not now. I, he, we spent one night together. I'm protected."

"Our Creator doesn't work on our schedule. You know how things work." Sage Cassie smiled with a soft laugh following. "We'll talk again soon."

Cassie stood looking at herself disbelieving but believing. She crawled into bed, face still wet with tears, and slept like the dead. Her phone ringing woke her. It was Vespa.

"Well finally." Vespa sounded concerned. Thought I was going to have to drive out there. You okay?"

Cassie shook the heavy sleep off just in time to rush to the toilet again.

"Cass, you okay?" She could hear Vespa over the speaker phone.

"Yeah, yeah. Just nerves."

"Poor Cass. Won't keep you long then. Things are a go with the Calhouns. Papers are signed on their end, and I've emailed them to you to sign. Need it tonight if you can get it done, doll."

"Sure, sure. Talk to me while I get to the computer. This will have no relation to GalUp, right?"

Vespa replied. "Not a thing. We had yet to incorporate that building into GalUp, but it was geared up to be the first building in the corporation, so you're safe. Although why, I have no idea. Providence I would say."

"Good. It may be all I have left." Cassie responded sadly.

"Don't believe that or speak that into existence. GalUp is yours and always will be."

"Vespa, I don't have control anymore. Someone screwed up, I pay the price."

"They can't do anything but fire you from working there. It's one share. We'll get it back."

Cassie e-signed the papers and returned them to Vespa, who noted that she had them. "Thanks, Vespa. See you tomorrow."

Cassie looked at the time. She had slept a good six hours. Feeling better, she ate some soup and read through the paperwork she brought home. She had until the end of the month to vacate as an employee of GalUp. That gave her until Sunday. She wept as she crawled back into bed.

Waking at 5 a.m., feeling decent, Cassie waited for her stomach to roll but got nothing. Breathing deeply, she poured some coffee and watched the sunrise before preparing for the day. She chose to leave a little early for a nice slow, contemplative drive back into Dallas. As she pulled into GalUp, she saw Vespa. They hugged and headed in, finding everyone including Drake in the conference room. Vespa acknowledged everyone as did Cassie.

Cassie suddenly remembered the face of the woman, Hannah Corbitt, but not from where. Hannah stood to speak, and Cassie held her hand up to silence her. She herself stood to speak. "While I am no longer majority shareholder, I still have a say and a vote. I will begin this meeting."

Hannah rustled her papers and glared at Cassie. Cassie pulled a package out while Vespa prepared something on the computer. "On the notice I received. Technically, as an employee, you have to prove incompetence to fire me. You will find nothing in my employee file showing that or any type of reprimand. If you fire me, I will sue."

Hannah bristled and attempted to speak again but was silenced by Cassie's hand a second time. "My attorney has informed me of my rights as an employee so if you find fault, now would be the best time to share them."

Hannah quickly stood. "Who is your attorney? We suggest he be at this meeting."

Cassie smiled. "She," emphasizing the word, "is here. Please, continue."

"That," Hannah pointed to Vespa, "is the corporation's attorney. She cannot represent you and us."

Vespa rose. Cassie saw her jaw clench, trying to keep her temper controlled. Placing her pen gently on the table, she spoke. "That, sent out her resignation two days ago. He," pointing to Drake, "accepted and hired another. You should read your email more often" She acknowledged a young man sitting next to Drake. "Jacob, good to see you."

Jacob nodded.

"You cannot do that!" Hannah exclaimed loudly, sending a hateful look Drake's way.

"Of course I can." Drake shot back. "I am a managing shareholder and board member. My contract has me stated as such.. That means I can hire and fire, accept resignations, and run this company to the best of my ability without having to hold a meeting every five minutes."

Hannah blustered and sat down, her face showing her disdain for the way the meeting was going.

"Please continue, Cassie." He motioned.

"So, without good reason, we find this notice to be void. Does anyone object?" No one spoke. "Then I will continue as an employee at GalUp until I chose not to."

Hannah stood yet again.

"I'm not finished. The empty building on the northeast corner of this block has been leased out and a joint venture with Calhoun Investments has been signed into contract."

"That will not happen. GalUp has already contracted it out." Hannah butted in.

"Oops." Cassie grinned. "That property has not been incorporated into GalUp. I own it personally. And more likely than not, I won't be asking for it to be incorporated. Hope you didn't put too much money into your venture.

Hannah angrily threw out, "We'll see about this! I want proof that it has not been incorporated."

At which Vespa threw a file down the table at her. "Started but not completed. The owner wouldn't sell to a corporation, so Cassie paid for it personally. Gotta love them old cowboys." Vespa drawled.

"That was pretty good." Cassie noted to Vespa.

Vespa took a slight bow. "Thank you, darlin'"

Hannah sputtered as she and the two men with her read through the papers. She sat back, crossing her arms. "Fine. You done?"

"Nope. Just one more thing." Cassie motioned to Vespa. "I've yet to understand why you dislike me much that you would try to sabotage all my work and my company, but it stops today. I have something I would like you see." As the video of the hall near her university office played, Cassie watched Hannah go white. Then realizing she was found out, sat quietly glaring at Cassie and Vespa. "You took advantage of a situation not related to GalUp and tried to ruin me." Cassie accused. "Why?"

"Because I could." Was the only reply.

Vespa harrumphed and ended it by slamming her computer shut. Cassie nodded and Vespa sat but was spring loaded and holding. "Hannah, I'm giving you every opportunity to explain before I press charges. And I have enough evidence to do so. You got careless and got caught. To my knowledge, I've never met you nor done anything wrong to you." Cassie looked Hannah over, pausing again to give her time to speak. "No defense? Nothing? You just decided one day to destroy my careers?"

As Cassie stood there looking at Hannah, she saw several emotions flicker across her face before the look of hatred settled back in. Vespa, having had enough, bolted out of her chair towards Hannah. "So, things will play this way now." Leaning over her. "You will either come clean, with explanation, you've been resigned from the board of GalUp, or I will pop this video and all the evidence, plus witness list over to the DA. You go to jail for a bit, our lives are good."

Hannah glared defiantly at Vespa, looking as if she wanted to punch her. She stood, causing Vespa to stand back, but not back down. She stepped away from her chair and walked to the opposite side of the table. Everyone expected her to walk out but she pulled a file from her bag instead. Tossing it on the table toward Cassie, Hannah returned to her chair and slowly leaned back. "Look at it."

Vespa returned to Cassie's side and both women quickly read through it. Cassie blanched toward the end and looked up with tears in her eyes. "But why?" Was all she could croak out.

"You haven't seen enough to figure it out?" Hannah snarked.

"I don't understand how you could do something like this to your own daughter." Cassie cried.

"Because you ignored me." Hannah informed her.

"What? I thought you were dead. Auntie Nev told me you left me on her door and went off to die somewhere. We never heard from you." Cassie said in shock.

"You never tried to look for me when you got older. When you turned 16, before she died, I tried to contact you. Letters, phone calls, even in person and was rejected at every turn."

Callie looked at Drake, who seemed as dumbfounded as she was. He shook his head no, telling Cassie silently he knew nothing. She dropped her eyes back to the folder but touched nothing.

Hannah continued. "Her estate knew before she died that I was alive. Hell, she knew as well. I asked for a meeting with her and you and was told no. Then she died, leaving everything to you. I filed for custody. That was thrown out of court. You needed someone to take care of you after her old ass died. You managed quite well, then you went to college, and I knew I'd lost."

"Why didn't you contact me after Auntie died?"

"They had turned you against me by then. I had a child out of wedlock. The father was not up to their standards. For that matter, guess I wasn't either."

"I never knew you to be turned against you. No one ever talked about you. Whatever you were told never came from me. And yet, you chose to destroy me instead of trying to connect?" Cassie asked, incredulous about the whole situation. "Wouldn't life have been easier that way?"

Hannah laughed. "For a princess, sure. For a pregnant half-breed, never."

Cassie head shot up. "Excuse me?"

"Your grandmother was unfaithful. It resulted in me. Father reminded me every day, but he took care of me. Although, it would have been nice to have seen just a tad of the inheritance he left. He left all $10 million to her, $10 thousand was all I got. A pittance."

Vespa cleared her throat. "Still doesn't explain all this shit." Pointing to the notes and video. "Why make Cassie pay?"

Hannah regarded the comment before replying. "Sins of the father."

"Holy hell!" Vespa threw her hands up in the air. "You tried to destroy her careers. You're trying to destroy her company. She had nothing to do with any of it."

Hannah's hands slapped down on the table. "She has everything to do with it. She ignored every attempt at contact. She didn't search for me. She's a stripper. She lives in my house."

"Your house? That belonged to her aunt." Vespa cut in.

"That bitch didn't love it the way I did, do. She sold the land around it after I requested she give it to me just so I couldn't claim any of it." Hannah snarled out. "I don't know how much is left, but the house should have been mine."

Cassie felt breathless and nauseous but was determined to get to the bottom of this insane declaration. Nothing had prepared her for this revelation. Looking at Drake, she knew he felt the same. She inhaled deeply, trying to settle her nausea. She held her hand to her head, furiously going through her memories to see if this woman ever tried to connect with her. She could find nothing. Her determination to end this made her speak with resolve.

"Fine. You were wronged. I get that. But your past has nothing to do with why you've attempted to destroy my career with the university and why you're forcing me out of GalUp."

The look of hatred Hannah shot Cassie caused her to gasp. She saw and knew in her mind then, this woman had come unhinged in her life and wanted others to pay for whatever wrong she felt had been done to her. Cassie didn't feel sorry for her, she felt scared for herself.

"When daddy died, I got nothing. $10,000. That was it. After everything that happened, I stayed right beside him. I vowed to destroy everything my sister inherited. She took the money, that corner lot building and created a piece of trash business. It grew and she made more money. She never offered to help me. Not one dime. I was destitute. I thought a husband would help, but as soon as I got pregnant, he left, taking everything. I worked at a club until you started showing. She had a house that sat empty. She could have given that to me. Nope. So, I gave you to her too. She wanted it all. She got it."

Tears fell as Cassie listened, not even noticing Vespa clacking away on her computer. Hannah continued. "When you inherited this building, rundown and dying, I prayed you would sell it. The end. But you had to follow in her footsteps." Hannah spat out. "You went to college. You became her. And it wasn't until you went public with shares that my plan came about. The university troubles were a fluke and one that almost worked to my advantage."

"You survived that only because I couldn't bribe that stupid boy. But I know enough people. I managed to put you on their radar. Then, when things calmed down there, they backed away. I ended up doing things myself. I was planning a big show for Friday that would have gotten you fired on the spot." She leaned forward, smirking. "Strippers would have enjoyed your little campus. Too bad most people have a conscience."

Vespa and Drake both shot out of their chairs. Drake spoke first. "Hannah, if anything happens on that campus, you will be in jail before they twitch one toe."

Hannah snickered. "The twain shall never meet. It was cancelled when Cassie let Tyler back on her staff. I didn't have a scapegoat. But I kept the notes going to keep things on everyone's mind until I knew for sure that door was closed." She looked Drake dead in the eye. "But I have control of GalUp and will see it comes to an end."

Drake never flinched or looked away. "You have shares, nothing more. You've been removed from the board."

"That is correct." Hannah acknowledged. "But I've implemented what I needed to see it fall and will continue to do so. As smart as you are, you should never have invited us to be on the board. It won't matter about the shares now."

"You would still see this fall?" Drake questioned. "Only GalUp was what you were after. There's so much more here now."

"And I'll see each business close because of GalUp now, piece by piece, slowly dying. Who wants a high-class business next to a sleazy strip joint?" The crazed look in her eyes told them this was true. "There's more than one way to destroy people."

Drake looked to the other shareholder/board members, one of whom responded, "We're with her."

"So, you're holding something over them as well. I see." He stayed standing, not willing to give up. "You won't have enough votes to sell, and I'll make sure no one wants to buy."

"Oh, there's ways around anything. Come Monday, GalUp will become a strip club." She laughed manically. "Shareholders voted that in. So, if your girl wants center stage, she'll have to flash 'em." Hannah giggled, pointing to her shimmying chest.

"I'll stop this!" Drake countered, at which point Cassie flung the folder down the table at Hannah, causing her to flinch away.

"You're crazy and so are your goons. Do what you want. I'll win in the end. I know people too. I'll get GalUp back. I've got time. More than you." Cassie spoke calmly, which surprised her. She then sat back, putting her feet on the table. A simple revelation had come to her. "We've all been so surprised and shocked today that we've forgotten basic business. Even you Ms. Destroy It All."

Hannah stopped to look at Cassie's sudden change. A confused look came over her face. "And that would be?"

"You're a shareholder only now. You have to have a majority vote to sell off anything, not just 51%. How you managed that 51% will be found out. But the point is, this, the original building and all the land and other buildings are still in my name. I own them. You knew that and that's why you tried to ruin me and are now trying to ruin GalUp. Well, guess what? Before that one itty bitty business goes, I will make sure everything else goes first." Cassie paused for effect. It worked. "And that will take a very long time. Bet your boobs on that."

Hannah sputtered, growing livid but saying nothing.

Cassie continued. "As for the changes made to GalUp, this place will close just like you want. People don't want to dine with T&A hanging all over the place. It won't be pretty, you'll lose a lot of money. But one thing will never change." She pointed to herself. "I will still own the buildings. I win. So do as you will. I'll be gone after Friday. As long as I get my money regularly, there will be no complaints. Losing money is not an option so you had better make sure you know what you're doing. I'll leave everything in Drake's capable hands. Unless he's fired too?" She threatened and questioned.

Hannah stood and gathered her things, her two sidekicks mimicking her. She didn't look completely defeated but enough to make Cassie happy. "As for the mother daughter connection, Auntie Nev was more mother than you could ever have hoped to be. No familial feelings here, only contempt. GalUp is yours for the time being, but rest assured, I'll get her back. At your expense."

Cassie had put her feet down and was now standing, moved to the door, opened it, and invited them out. "You know the way. Don't let the door hit you in the ass on the way out."

After they left, Cassie felt totally drained. She gulped water as she listened to Vespa, Drake, and Jacob but didn't really hear what was being said until Vespa nudged her. She jolted to attention. Vespa had been searching Hannah's background through another source and was trying to keep her temper controlled. She had found that despite some rough living in her younger days, she had managed to earn a degree in corporate management and had bought and sold many businesses over the years.

Upon sending out some emails, the quick replies showed the two men had known each of the owners of the businesses long before the purchase and resale and that there were suggestions that some shady happenings were behind those sales. Vespa had sent her PI out almost immediately to investigate.

They all agreed that something, somewhere in their dealings didn't seem right. Drake scheduled time with the accountant to go back through records and research. He was not happy. Jacob and Vespa assured him that they would figure it all out. Vespa had taken photos of the folder Hannah had shared and she and Jacob moved to the end of the table to review it. Cassie sighed contently, feeling safe. She touched Drake's hand, picturing his gentleness despite the size. "How would he handle a child?" She mused.

"Drake." She broke the silence.

"Mm-hmm."

"We do need to talk but give me until Saturday. Come after the night is over. I'll be waiting."

Drake squeezed Cassie's hand and agreed. She gathered her things, said her goodbyes, and headed to her home, needing the drive to think.

Chapter 12

As she hit the outskirts of town, a thought crossed her mind, and she turned back. Back at GalUp, she headed to the one apartment that had never been remodeled. Auntie Nev's office/bedroom. She went through the desk and drawers, knowing but not knowing what she was looking for. Then she saw it, an old photograph book with more surrounding it, hidden by boxes. In the boxes were journals dating back to her auntie's youth. Cassie had never looked at the photos after high school, nor read the journals. She had forgotten about them as she worked on her future. Hoping not to be noticed, she managed to get them all into her car and headed back out.

Once home and unloaded, Cassie texted Tyler about teaching her classes until Monday, informed her regent as well, stating a personal matter had come up, and set about really learning of her Auntie Nev's life. She hoped maybe to find out a bit about her birth mother as well.

She dated the journals with the photograph books and once done, decided to eat and shower before diving in. She saw herself in the mirror. Then Maiden Cassie popped in, blew her a kiss, and changed into her second self. Enchantress Cassie gave her a sexy wink then changed to Sage Cassie, her regular self.

"It's official. I'm as looney as my looney mother." She spoke out loud.

"Well, it's a possibility, but I highly doubt it. She's a total lunatic." Sage Cassie rolled her eyes, causing the real Cassie to giggle. "What a day!"

"You're not kidding!" Cassie agreed. At least I didn't puke all day. Is that going to be a thing?"

Sage Cassie smiled. "Only for a couple of days and then you're good to go. You'll find yourself with odd cravings though. I was hoping not to have those."

Cassie rolled her eyes, causing Sage Cassie to smile this time. "Oh, joy."

Sage Cassie raised her palms and cocked her head. "Oh well, it is what it is. Now, let's talk. Take a seat."

Cassie went to the mirror on her bedside table, turned it to face her, finding Sage Cassie patiently waiting. "So... how did your day go?" Sage Cassie spoke, jiggling her head side to side, grinning.

"I really hope you're kidding." Cassie didn't laugh or even smile. "I'm not rehashing."

"Darling, been there, burned the t-shirt. You survived. That's all that matters."

"I don't want to "survive" again." Cassie commented, using air quotes.

"I'll just say, the horrible worst is almost over. You'll start a new chapter after Friday."

Cassie snorted then felt a calm assurance flow through her. She relaxed back into her chair.

"You're going to be an amazing person. Hell, you already are. Look at all you just accomplished. Starlight and stilettos made you the person you are. And the Creator of course. Feel proud. As you go through the past now, laugh, cry, get pissed, and forgive. You'll feel yourself healing and looking forward to your future."

Cassie felt tears prick her eyes and her throat grew tight. She cleared both with a cough and swipe. "I just wish the becoming didn't come with so much heartache." She whispered.

"Some do, some don't. But we survive and move forward, just like you are doing."

Cassie felt another wave of calm. "You have two days to go through a lifetime of someone's memories. Don't be swayed by needing to do something else. Learn." And Sage Cassie was replaced by the real Cassie.

Cassie sat and gave the day a thought. Just a quick review, remembering afterwards of feeling Drake's arm around her. She wondered if there would be more of those moments or would she be going life alone. Shaking the mood, Cassie put on extra comfy clothes and headed to her living room and her auntie's past.

Several hours later, feeling stiff and dusty, Cassie paused to get fresh water and stretch. She had spent over six hours reading and looking at photos, learning how her auntie was raised and was roughly one-third of the way through. It didn't seem like a bad life, just cautious. Not starting wealthy but affluent enough. Their wealth came soon after their daughters reached adulthood.

Engaged formally, Auntie's fiancé ended up dying right before going off to war, leaving her saddened. Quickly recovering, she was courted by a jazz player whom her parents did not approve of. She left town to travel with him. They were not married.

While her father did not disown her, he restricted her income until she returned. He forced her to work in his store as punishment. Hannah, the younger daughter, had been left to deal with the father who hated her and mother that didn't care. Auntie Nev refused to marry any man her father introduced her to and there were many. To Cassie's surprise, Auntie Nev had not mentioned sleeping with any of the men she met, including the jazz player. She remained untouched until her 40s, just like Cassie.

The man she finally gave herself to managed her father's store and thought relations with her would get him the place when her father died. It did not. He disappeared from Auntie Nev's life. Auntie, it seemed to Cassie, was a bit of a rebel. She never mentioned her younger sister except to note that the girl was obsessed with being the boss over everything and acted crazy like her real daddy, whom she had met a couple of times. Then only one other notation about her coming back for money.

Cassie stepped outside for fresh air, noting how bright the stars seemed and turned to the barn where her telescope was. "No." She told herself, "Get back to the past."

Cassie grabbed some snacks and water and resumed her journey of her auntie's life. Around 2 a.m. she curled up on the sofa and slept a dreamless sleep. Her phone woke her around 9 a.m. Vespa had called her several times. She answered.

"You're gonna force me out to that place one day!" Vespa joked. "Turn your ringer up, please."

"Cassie laughed. "What's up, lady lawyer?"

"Well, just the fact that your mommy dearest and her buddies have destroyed a lot of people she thought had wronged her in some way. Hardest part is getting the proof before she does it to you."

"Damn. How did no one see this?" Cassie asked.

"That's what her two bird dogs are for. Seems one is good at convincing people to go public with shares, getting them to use their people to set things up, then managing to get controlling interest."

Cassie felt her anger flare. "And we were sucked in as well."

"Pretty as you please, myself included. If we get enough evidence about this from other companies, we might be able to get the DA or even the FEDS involved. We're trying. But that's not why I called." Vespa paused.

Cassie breathed heavily, afraid to ask but did anyway. "So?"

"So." Vespa spit out quickly. "She put an ad in the newspapers about the changes at GalUp."

Cassie gasped. "Can she do that?"

"Not really, but it's done. Probably before she was fired from the board. And until we get things figured out, she's not gonna stop. Drake is running ragged trying to squash it and not having much luck."

Cassie wanted to go to GalUp. She said as much but Vespa warned her off. "She timed this hoping you would, which might connect you to the university. Let it ride."

"But I'm performing Friday. I cannot give into her." Cassie felt herself getting angry.

"Then don't. Kill the night. Make it one to remember. Just stay away until then. You're a professor, let her think your stars are more important than GalUp. Drake can handle things and I'll keep you in the loop as well." Vespa told her, trying to keep the conversation light.

"Damn that woman! Why so much hatred? An old building and a few million dollars." Cassie lamented.

"Maybe it wasn't and isn't about the money. Legally, she was your grandfather's daughter, so she had rights. But his will was solid. Who knows in this case. I say hatred at her life growing up and more after her father died and for not being recognized." Vespa explained.

Cassie paused and looked at the memorabilia in front of her. She thanked Vespa, telling her she had some work to finish and went back to reading, praying for answers. The day was a blur as she read and looked through photos. Even as she neared the end, Cassie had no answers. She saw her youth in the photos, her times at GalUp, and trips they took together.

Wednesday night saw her looking out the dark windows, still no closer but understanding why Auntie Nev was like she was. She fell asleep on the sofa, surrounded by her history but still feeling a void. A piece of the puzzle was missing. She was too tired to continue.

Dawn broking, finding Cassie drinking coffee and nibbling toast. Her mind going through everything, filing, noting, trying to piece it with what was happening now. She could see the pile in her living room and childishly stuck her tongue out at them.

Then, as if mocking her, the largest photo book toppled to the floor, scattering its contents. Cassie walked up to the mess, gathering the bits and pieces. As she lifted the book, she noticed a tear that had puffed out. Something was inside. Pulling the cloth back, two books dropped to the floor. One full of pictures, the other another journal.

Excitement coursed through Cassie and the tiredness she felt vanished. She returned to the kitchen with both books. Three hours later found her crying and angry at the same time, both with her grandparents and her mother. Cassie drew a breath and decided to shower before calling Vespa. Drake had enough to deal with so she would call him later.

"Well," Sage Cassie appeared in the mirror, "I'm feeling indignation or just good old fashion pissed off."

"Yes." Cassie replied.

"Now you know. But remember, their lives, not yours."

"Yeah. And it's affecting my life now. It's got to end." She paused. "I hope it will with me. I'm the last of the line."

"Mm-hmm." Sage Cassie nodded, not looking convinced.

"Oh God!" Cassie cried out. "What did I miss? Do I have a twin or something?"

"Or something." Sage Cassie answered.

"But you're not going to tell me, right?"

"I'm just here to guide you." And disappeared.

"Crapola! What the ever-frigging hell is going on? I just want my company back and to live my life without battling the whole damn state of Texas." Cassie growled as she stomped back to the living room.

Picking through the piles, she really had no clue what she was looking for. But then something clicked, and she opened the photo book that began the year she was born. Only a birth certificate with the father listed. Flipping through, nothing jumped out. Until it did. Toddler years, there are two children. The journal held no clue that she could find so she checked the panels again, finding a tiny slit. That slit revealed a birth certificate. Boy. Mother, Auntie Nev named. No father. "Holy moly, I have more family."

Cassie shot a picture and sent it to Vespa, giving her 24 hours to find what she could. Vespa replied positively, but also sent back a shot of a certain finger of her hand. Cassie giggled as she went back to reading through the papers, of which she also sent copies to Vespa.

The child of Auntie Nev was adopted out by her father. No records that Auntie Nev was able to find, and the courts had them sealed. Being heartbroken, when Cassie's mother became unable to take care of her, Auntie Nev took her. Cassie wept for the lives that had been destroyed by this. Maybe that's why her mother hated them both.

Early afternoon Thursday saw all the books repacked and hauled to a bedroom. Cassie would keep them close for now, in case of a new revelation. She had checked every cover for more surprises as she packed them. Nothing.

Her phone rang showing the caller as Vespa, who just dumped all the information she had out. "Your cousin is alive and well. He lives in the Fort Worth area. Lots of money and..." Cassie held her breath as Vespa paused, "your mother lives with him."

Cassie dropped onto a chair feeling sick. "You have a photo?" At which her phone dinged. It was of one of the men from the meeting.

"Cassie girl," Vespa broke the silence, "You okay? Do I need to come out?"

Cassie shook off the shock before answering. "No, no. I'm okay. Stunned. Saddened. I'll be fine. Come tomorrow night to GalUp."

Vespa confirmed and they disconnected. Cassie curled up on the sofa and cried. Hard, ugly crying. She didn't know how long she lay there, sobbing off and on, but a hand on her shoulder startled her as she was scooped up and nestled in a warm embrace, causing the tears to start again. As she calmed, Cassie looked up at Drake. "I told you not to come." She admonished.

Drake agreed with her statement. "You did. Vespa called and sounded desperate about you being alone. I didn't hesitate to come."

Cassie snuggled closer. "Thank you, Drake. It feels good like this. Right somehow. How did we not see it years ago?"

"Babe, I think I've known since the moment I met you. I knew you needed time to fly and become. You did. How even more beautiful you look to me right now."

Cassie snorted. "Yeah, right. Red nose, blotchy eyes."

"An angel."

Cassie couldn't have felt more loved or loved more than she did at that very moment. If not for the urge to pee, she would have stayed as long as possible.

"Babe, shower and relax. We'll just enjoy the evening. No pressure for anything other than company." Drake spoke sincerely. He just needed to be near her tonight. He had been driving to her when Vespa called.

The draw was not something he could explain. He was working and heard her calling, stopped dead, and left. On the drive he thought again about the meeting, the revelations, and what he had learned from Vespa. He didn't think she would do anything desperate, but he knew he had to be with her tonight. At least he knew the changed combination to the gate to get in. His birthday. When he found her curled on the sofa sobbing, he felt intense relief. When he touched her, his body relaxed. As he held her, his world felt complete. He let her cry until the tears subsided. His heart swelled with love.

While she showered, he hunted her kitchen to make dinner. It felt good to be doing something personal for her, even if it was just a small dish. Drake knew in his heart, she was his and he would do whatever it took to prove it to her. Getting to work, he began to whistle softly.

Cassie stood in front of the bathroom mirror, trying to get the redness out of her eyes. She looked like crap.

"No, you looked cleansed." Sage Cassie interrupted.

Snorting, Cassie replied. "Death warmed over."

"The question is, how do you feel?"

"Like I've been rung out." She thought for a second. "But I feel settled mostly. At least I know why and how. Doesn't make what they're doing right but now I can face things better." Cassie sighed shakily.

Sage Cassie smiled warmly, and Cassie felt a soothing calm wash over her. "And you've got a good man waiting downstairs."

"That too."

"So, spend the time wisely. Enjoy the company and just be."

"I don't know if I can but sounds like that's what he wants as well."

Cassie smiled at her Sage self and left the room, confident about herself once again. As she neared the kitchen, she heard Drake's soft whistle and smelled great things wafting out of the kitchen. "Do not enter this room!" Drake warned. "Go, sit. I'll be right out."

Cassie obeyed. The living room was her second most comfortable place and that's where she ended up. Drake soon followed, a tray loaded with delicious smells in his hands. Placing it on the table, he handed her a plate fully loaded, his small dish had expanded. Her stomach chose that moment to growl. Drake laughed, Cassie blushed.

They ate in companionable silence, just living in the moment. Cassie chose juice over wine, not knowing if she was really pregnant or not but didn't want to chance anything. They cleaned up together then sat outside to watch the sunset and finally drifted back inside to share the sofa. Cassie snuggled into the crook of Drake's arm, both feeling content and whole.

A few minutes later, Cassie started to talk, telling Drake everything. She talked about her other selves, most of their conversations, and all of the things she found in her auntie's journals, finishing with her feelings for him. "I do love you, Drake. Probably have since the day I met you as well, I was just too stupid to know it." She spoke softly.

"So, you have a split personality. Well, that ought to make for interesting conversations." He joked.

Cassie giggled. "You should have heard some of them."

Drake sat rubbing her arm and began his side of the story. All his doubts, fears, struggles, as well as triumphs. He told her how he watched her grow, how he was afraid she would outgrow him, finding another to love. As he talked about GalUp and the situation, tears flowed. He apologized repeatedly for missing the change. The pain in his voice caused Cassie to snuggle even closer, assuring him everything would work out.

"It was you, wasn't it?" She asked Drake.

"Me what?" He replied.

"You are my benefactor for the research funding. You sent the note."

"Mm-hmm."

"I love you."

They talked about future plans, her career at the university, how they would handle GalUp, and her new venture in the stars. She brought up maybe doing something with the ranch, claiming a new adventure was waiting for them. He told her he would love that and check into what she had explained about wanting. At 2 a.m. as they dosed in each other's arms, Vespa called. Cassie put her on speaker.

"We can get them!" She spoke excitedly." It's gonna take a while to gather all the evidence and witnesses. I don't know what they'll do with GalUp in the meantime. They've seized control, have majority vote, but I'll do my best to hold off anything they try."

"And if they get past you, then what?" Drake questioned.

"That's where you and Jacob come in."

"Excuse me?" Drake again questioned.

Vespa took a deep breath. "You'll have to find ways or reasons to stall. Hannah wants the oldest building. The clothing store in her mind. She's gonna try anything to get it, including ruining all the other businesses associated with GalUp."

Cassie perked up. "But I own the building. That means she'll go after me as well."

"Yep. You need to talk to the other business owners/investors and especially the university people. Short and sweet but talk. You've got three days left but today is when it needs to be done. And even though things might be settled in some areas, the possibility for failure is there."

"Daylight, I'll be out." Cassie told her.

Vespa was agitated but assured Cassie and Drake. "Me and my team are full on this. I want that witch, and I want her bad, but I have to do this legally. The DA is aware of things and waiting."

Cassie thanked Vespa, telling her to keep them updated. Drake thanked her as well. The two, without asking each other, went to bed and slept until Tyler phoned at dawn. He told them his father had been contacted about rehashing the mess from Tennessee. After explaining the situation a bit, Cassie contacted her regent and texted Tyler to have his father meet them at that office.

"On it, boss." Tyler replied with a smile emoji.

CHAPTER 13

As they drove to Dallas together, Drake said he'd drop her off and see her at GalUp later. They kissed goodbye as Tyler and his father drove up. Cassie shook hands and they spent the next two hours with her regent, explaining her situation. The regent seemed understanding and claimed her job was secure. If anyone posted anything anywhere or phone calls were received, she would be contacted. Tyler went to class and his father dropped her off at Vespa's.

There, they went through information, contacts, and tried to make a game plan of sorts. Hannah had hidden things very well and unearthing it all was a challenge and chore. "We're looking at months before we can do anything." Vespa told Callie, exasperated. "Only saving grace is any sale she attempts now will take a while. She's on radar. Hopefully, Drake and Jacob will be kept in the loop."

"That woman is insane. Did you see the notice in the paper? She's going to ruin GalUp's reputation."

"Only for a little while. But we're fighting that as well. We can only hope for something big to drop soon." Vespa told her.

"Three days won't be soon enough for me." Cassie growled. Then, noticing the clock, started for the door. "You will be there?"

"With bells on. But not for dancing." Vespa cocked her hips, Cassie laughed.

As the taxi drove to GalUp, doubts and fears filled her once again. Sadness creeped into her. Tears filled her eyes. On the way, she stopped at a pharmacy and bought a pregnancy test, being congratulated by the clerk.

Two hours to kill, she snuck into Auntie Nev's apartment and took the test. Sage was right. Pregnant. Cassie giggled nervously. She sat at Auntie's desk, contemplating. Emotions ran through her, making her feel like she was on a roller coaster. As she gazed around the room, she spotted a journal she missed sitting by the bed. It had one entry addressed to her.

"My Darling Cassandra,

I fear for what your future holds. You're just coming into your own and I might have set you up for failure leaving you this place. Don't try to save it. Sell it. Take the best offer and run. Your future is in the stars, not stilettos. GalUp has had an amazing run, but she's tired, just like me.

I know you know nothing of your past. Probably a good thing. Your momma was declared insane medically just before you were born. That's why you were taken away from her as mine was taken away from me. Where I couldn't find him, I did find you. I love you more than you know.

If you've not found the other journals, you need to so you'll understand your history. You're good blood. I know that in my heart. You won't follow in your momma's footsteps if I can help it. Use the strength passed down to make life work for you.

Your momma claims she will make everyone who hurt her pay. In her mind, it's most anyone she's ever been in contact with. I should have had her committed, but I didn't. For that, I'm sorry. You have a cousin out there somewhere. I don't know where, as I couldn't get the courts to unseal the records. Maybe he'll be an ally if he's been told of his real family.

Cassandra my daughter, I gave it all to you to live happily ever after. Build a good life and never look back.

Auntie Nev"

Cassie felt the tears, but they were of joy. Her heart was saddened by the events of her auntie and mother's past. She now understood her auntie but still not her mother. She phoned Drake and he flew through the door.

"I was worried again. Vespa said you were coming here but you never showed." He spoke between pants, trying to catch his breath.

"I had something to confirm." She told him. "There is one more journal." Handing it to Drake.

He read through and sat down. The weight he felt lifted, and he reached out to Cassie. She reached back but stayed in her chair opposite him. "But that's not the only confirmation I got today."

"Oh? What else?" he asked.

Cassie felt trepidation, but knew honesty was the best. "I'm pregnant."

Drake flushed with a look of surprise. "From one night?"

"Apparently one time is all it takes." She laughed nervously.

"Holy moly! Boy or girl?" Drake was grinning from ear to ear.

Cassie grinned back. "Little early to determine that, Drake. I'm only three-and-a-half weeks along."

Then they were in each other's arms, laughing like school kids. Drake's phone buzzed. He had to go. Cassie roamed the room one last time before heading to her dressing room, journal in hand.

As she walked through the club, Cassie knew this was her last dance. She had no idea how she was going to please the already growing crowd. Not many recognized her under her scarf but those that did waved excitedly to her. Walking to the sound booth, she perused her music list. Nothing seemed right. Thomas asked her if anything was wrong, and she mumbled something to him. "You know what, Thomas? I'm lost as to what to do tonight. You pick it. I'll make it up as I go."

Thomas looked at Cassie stunned and confused. Not once in all the past years had she ever asked him to pick her music. "You sure, Cass? It's not something I've ever done for you."

She nodded. "I'm just feeling," searching for a word, "lost and small." I don't know what's wrong or what fits my mood. Just hook me up." And walked out, leaving Thomas perturbed.

It hit him. He messaged her what he thought she should wear and made his notes on how he wanted the crew to work the lighting. Where Cassie was confused, the fates helped Thomas to make a queen that night.

Cassie stood looked at the crowd in GalUp that normally filled Friday nights. This crowd seemed different. Very high rollers from Dallas and Fort Worth. It was as if they were anticipating something. But what? Probably the ad in the newspaper drawing them to see if she stripped.

She saw Drake chatting it up with Jake Erickson, an oil guy from Midland and his legal team. Questions filled her mind. He kept glancing at the mirror as if he knew she was standing there. She wondered what that conversation was about.

"Enough!" She cried out loud. "I'm done. Everyone wins." She noticed her message from Thoms as she threw herself on the sofa. "Why that?" She asked to no one. "The oldest and first outfit?" But rose to find it tucked away in the back of her closet.

Cassie sat in front of her mirror, not feeling like Lady Cassandra at all. All of the info she had discovered, all of the confirmations of her other selves, all of the battles she had faced since that day in Tennessee, felt like 20 tons weights pressing on her shoulders. But then she thought, how could she walk away and leave this life? It was part of who she was.

She applied soft makeup. Highlights that made her not look her 45 years but instead, like an 18-year-old just starting out in life. She pulled her hair away from her face tonight, securing it with a set of pins Drake had gifted her in college. As usual, her face glowed as if kissed by the sun. The dress was an ensemble that fit her body snugly but allowed for movement from any angle. The soft gold and green hues accentuating her skin and hair. She looked innocent.

Thomas texted Cassie to go to the shelf, meaning she was starting from above instead of below tonight. She sighed, hoping he knew what he was doing because she sure as hell didn't. Makeup and dress complete, she stepped into her dance shoes, gold stilettos with green accents and then stepped over to the window again. Drake was still at the table she'd seen him at earlier, looking to be deep in conversation. The moment she stepped to the window though, he looked up, giving her chills as to how he seemingly knew she was there. "Are you a traitor?" She thought silently. "Will I be alone after tonight?"

"Twenty minutes" Came the text from Thomas. "Only two songs tonight. They will be enough."

Cassie took the deepest breath she could as she scanned the crowd, then closed them trying to relax as she just breathed. She began the short trek to the shelf as Thomas began her countdown. He spoke as she walked. "Was she calm, cool, and beautiful?" he asked. She laughed, calling him crazy. The crew helped her onto the platform and connected her safety straps. They all saluted her silently and stepped away to give her privacy to prepare. Thomas gave the ten-minute announcement.

"Ladies and gentlemen, Lady Cassandra will be sharing her final performance at GalUp tonight." "How did he know that?" Cassie wondered. "If you have had the honor, privilege, and pleasure of seeing her perform, you know she is mesmerizing and hypnotizing. Tonight, Lady Cassandra will stun you with a farewell performance that will leave you breathless as well as speechless. Be prepared to view this final and most amazing performance of Lady Cassandra's career at GalUp. In ten minutes, you will be unable to look away from center stage."

Drake started at this announcement. He knew something had happened but never thought Cassie would walk away from GalUp. Leaving the table was not an option at this point, neither was a text as

Cassie would not have her phone. He would just have to wait it out like everyone else.

Cassie heard but was beginning to close out all noise from her jumbled mind. She focused on her body, feeling it tune and become taunt, ready to move. Still not knowing what song Thomas chose, she hummed softly to keep her mind on the next few standby minutes.

When her time arrived, the only warning she got was Thomas announcing her. "Ladies and gentlemen, I give you Lady Cassandra."

The lights never changed so she had no time to completely compose herself. She closed her eyes and took a deep breath. A single simple flute melody filled the hushed house. Not a sound could be heard. That flute caused Cassie's heart to quicken. "No! I can't!" But as the lights softened to a dusky hue and the platform began its descent, a voice softly spoke. "Yes. You can."

Cassie became nervous and felt very small, so she curled inward as she came into view of GalUp's audience. Her chest tightened, and her breath caught, each step forward feeling like a trek through thick, clinging fog. The stage lights were blinding, casting a harsh glare that illuminated her every movement, every trembling breath. She felt exposed, as if the weight of every gaze could pierce through her carefully constructed facade. A soft gasp broke the tension. It was so faint it could have come from the audience, or perhaps it escaped her own lips, an involuntary reaction to the overwhelming intensity of the moment. Cassie couldn't tell. All she knew was the sensation of her heart pounding like a drum inside her chest.

The flute continued its haunting melody, echoing through her mind as well as the room. The sound was otherworldly, like a phantom's whisper curling around her, weaving its way into the very marrow of her being. Each note lingered in the air, a delicate, trembling thread that connected her to something larger than herself. Its tendrils slowly eased the tightness in her chest, replacing fear with a quiet, creeping calm. She felt its music seep into her veins, filling her with a strange, hypnotic rhythm. As the platform lowered her to the main stage, Cassie allowed herself to unfurl slowly, like a tightly wound bud opening to the warmth of the sun. Her steps were hesitant, each one more assured than the last. The cables unhooked with a soft click, releasing her, and as the haunting flute gave way to a new pulse of sound, her senses awakened. This was her stage, her arena, and her truth waiting to be claimed. Her song, her fragmented selves, her very life seemed to linger just beyond the edge of the stage lights, urging her forward to take hold.

Cassie began the sensual moves as the Virgin self filled her eyes and mind. Her body moved with the youthful exuberance of a girl just discovering the thrill of her own existence. Her hips swayed in playful arcs, her arms reaching out as if grasping at unseen dreams. The Virgin was untamed and curious, her every motion an exploration, a question posed to the universe. She danced with the innocence of one who had yet to feel the weight of the world, her steps quick and light, as if she might take flight at any moment. Cassie could feel the boundless energy of this self coursing through her, a girl eager to escape the dull confines of routine, to embrace the unknown with open arms. Together, they spun and swayed, their movements synchronizing in perfect harmony until, with a burst of light, they converged. Cassie felt the closure of this chapter, a sense of fulfillment, as the Virgin self dissolved into her being.

The Enchantress self glided around, dancing a dance of seduction and desire, leaving a trail of breathlessness in her wake. Her movements were slow, deliberate, and intoxicating, each step a calculated temptation. Cassie's eyes flashed with confidence as she embodied the Enchantress, a woman in her prime who wielded her power like a weapon. Her hands skimmed over her body, tracing curves that drew the audience's gaze like moths to a flame. She twirled, her hair fanning out, a sensual storm that left her audience spellbound. The Enchantress was unapologetic in her desires, her every gesture a declaration of sovereignty. She commanded attention, exuding a magnetic allure that could captivate any heart. Together, Cassie and the Enchantress danced with a shared purpose, to own their space, to claim their desires. The two selves fused in a powerful moment of self-acceptance, a celebration of the woman she had become.

The Sage self, her now self, full of knowledge, bearing life, stepped forward with gentle authority. Her movements slowed, each one deliberate, imbued with a sense of calm and wisdom. The Sage moved with the grace of a river, steady and unwavering, her arms flowing outward as if gathering the audience into her embrace. Cassie felt the weight of this self, the comforting presence of a woman who had weathered life's storms and emerged stronger, wiser. The Sage danced in widening circles, her feet barely touching the floor, as if she carried the wisdom of ages with her. Her dance spoke of peace and a deep, abiding love that transcended time. She reached inward, drawing Cassie into the safety of her nurturing arms, whispering of new beginnings and the beauty of a life fully lived. Together, they moved in perfect harmony, their souls intertwining as the Sage offered her blessings of grace and renewal.

As Cassie turned, a final spin brought her face-to-face with her mother self. This was the culmination of her journey, the woman she would one day become, who had taught her patience and resilience. The Mother self was a vision of seasoned beauty, her face lined with the wisdom of years but still aglow with the vitality of youth. Her hands, soft yet strong, reached out to Cassie, inviting her into a dance of reflection and joy. Together, they swayed and spun, their movements slow and rhythmic, weaving through the music as if threading their shared history into the fabric of the moment. Cassie felt a deep sense of peace as the Mother self guided her through memories of love, sacrifice, and triumph. As the music swelled to its crescendo, the Mother began to fade, her form retreating into the shadows. But before she disappeared, she whispered softly, her voice carrying the weight of infinite love: "My time is not yet."

Cassie danced a dance not of seduction but of freedom. Her body moved with a fluidity that spoke of release, each motion shedding the weight of doubts and disappointments. She spun faster, her arms slicing through the air, her legs pounding the stage with defiance. The battles she had fought, the struggles she had endured, flashed before her like fleeting shadows, powerless against the force of her determination. Her dance became a declaration of wholeness, a celebration of the woman she had fought to become. She felt the bonds of fear and uncertainty breaking, falling away like chains shattered by the sheer force of her will. Cassie was free, her spirit unburdened and soaring.

As the song came to a single note of the flute, Cassie knew how full her future life would be. She stood still for a moment, letting the final note linger in the air, a delicate thread that connected her to the infinite possibilities ahead. Slowly, she placed her hands over her abdomen, a symbolic gesture of rebirth and renewal. She opened her arms wide, her body unfolding like a flower blooming in the first warmth of spring. The music faded, leaving behind a profound silence that seemed to stretch endlessly.

Opening her eyes, she noted not a sound, not a breath, just soft sobs and tears glistening in the stage lights. The audience was transfixed, their emotions laid bare by the raw vulnerability of her performance. Cassie felt their connection, a shared understanding of the struggles and triumphs that defined the human experience. Her gaze swept the room, and she realized Drake's seat was empty. Yet, even this did not trouble her. In this moment, Cassie had found the answers she had been seeking. She had danced through her fears, embraced her selves, and emerged whole. She was no longer searching for validation or fulfillment outside herself. Cassie knew that her journey was far from over, but for the first time, she felt at peace with the woman she was becoming and the life that lay ahead.

Ten minutes later, the lights in the club dimmed, casting an almost ethereal glow over the stage. A soft spotlight appeared, illuminating her lone figure. Cassie stepped into it slowly, her silhouette both mysterious and alluring. The faint notes of a slow, sultry jazz piece began to play, low bass, a whispering saxophone, and the gentle caress of piano keys. The music seemed to wrap around her like a velvet glove, inviting the audience into her world.

Cassie wore a costume that mirrored the cosmos itself. A deep midnight blue corset adorned with tiny, sparkling crystals mimicked a starry sky. The boning of the corset accentuated her curves, leaving her shoulders and arms bare. A sheer skirt of dark tulle flowed around her legs, slit high on one side, revealing long, thigh-high stockings with garters that glinted under the lights.

On her feet, a pair of towering stilettos, silver and encrusted with rhinestones that caught the light with every movement. Her hair cascaded in loose, sultry waves, adorned with a delicate headpiece resembling a crescent moon. Beneath her corset, glimpses of lace and satin teased the audience, leaving just enough to the imagination to drive them wild.

Cassie began with a single, deliberate step forward, her hips swaying in time with the languid beat. She lifted her gloved hands above her head, letting them trace a slow, sinuous line down her body, pausing just above the curve of her hips. The audience was entranced, their eyes locked on her every move. Her gaze was heavy-lidded, lips curved in a knowing, secretive smile as she made eye contact with various patrons, drawing them into her orbit.

She moved with feline grace, her stilettos clicking softly against the stage. With every step, every turn, she exuded confidence and sensuality, her body speaking a language of seduction. She turned her back to the audience, glancing over her shoulder, giving them a playful wink before rolling her hips in a slow figure-eight motion. The sheer fabric of her skirt shifted, revealing the toned lines of her legs, tantalizing glimpses of her stockings and garters.

The music began to shift, the tempo subtly increasing. The saxophone grew bolder, more insistent, as if urging her forward. Cassie hooked her thumbs under the straps of her corset and, with an artful shrug of her shoulders, let the first layer of her gloves slide down her arms. She spun, the tulle skirt flaring out like a galaxy in motion, before stopping abruptly, facing the audience with a fierce, commanding stare.

One glove fell to the floor. Then the other. She draped the edge of her skirt over her fingers, lifting it slightly to reveal the tops of her stockings, and then let it fall again, a tease that left the audience breathless. The music swelled as she moved to the edge of the stage, leaning in close enough for the front-row patrons to feel the heat of her presence.

The piano grew louder, more dramatic, joined by a pulsing drumbeat that set a fiery, urgent pace. Cassie matched the intensity of the music, her movements became sharper, more commanding. She unhooked her corset with a single, decisive motion, revealing a sparkling bra beneath that gleamed like the Milky Way. The crowd erupted in applause, their energy feeding her own.

She danced with abandon now, spinning, kicking, and striking powerful poses. Each motion was deliberate, every step an assertion of her control and power. The skirt came loose, fluttering to the floor like a falling comet, leaving her in the shimmering, starlit lingerie that clung to her body. Her stilettos added an edge of danger to her every step, making her appear both untouchable and magnetic.

Cassie slid down to her knees, arching her back as the music reached its fever pitch. The drums were pounding, the sax wailing in wild ecstasy. She flipped her hair, tossing her head back as she crawled across the stage, each movement slow, deliberate, like a predator stalking her prey. Her hands traveled along her thighs, her waist, up her body, emphasizing every curve.

As Cassie danced, her heart pounded not just from exertion but from the sheer power she felt. Every step, every sway of her hips, was a reclamation of her own story. The stage was her sanctuary, her battlefield, her temple. She felt the eyes on her, but instead of shrinking under their gaze, she thrived. She commanded their attention, their admiration, their awe.

In those moments under the spotlight, she channeled the energy of every woman who had ever fought to reclaim her space in the world. She felt connected to something ancient, something wild and untamed, as if the very stars are dancing with her. And when the final applause roared through the room, Cassie knew she was not just a performer, she was a force of nature, unstoppable, unapologetically herself.

As the music reached its dramatic climax, Cassie rose to her feet in a single, fluid motion. She twirled once more, throwing her arms out as if to embrace the audience. The lights flashed in sync with the final, thunderous beat of the drums. She struck her final pose, one arm lifted high, the other draped across her waist, her head tilted back as if bathing in the light of an unseen star.

The stage lights dim once again, leaving only a faint glow as the last notes of the music fade into silence. For a moment, there is nothing but the sound of heavy breathing, hers and the audience's, as they process the sheer intensity of what they've just witnessed.

After a final bow and a kiss blown to Thomas, Cassie walked front center stage and traveled down the steps through the silent tables and to the open doors of GalUp. She may wear stilettos, but she walked like a queen, each step echoing with the power of a woman who has truly come into her own. Her heart caught in her throat when she saw Drake standing in the doorway with her case and coat. No words were spoken as she approached him.

Drake helped her with her coat, and she smiled up at him, holding his gaze. She then held out her hand and felt intense love when he took it in his. They gazed into each other's eyes and walked out of GalUp, neither hearing the applause that sounded as if it was bringing the roof down.

PROLOGUE

Six months later, Cassie and Drake were contacted by the controlling shareholders of GalUp. After Cassie left and the strippers came into GalUp to perform, the financial loss was almost devastating. Losing money and clientele, Hannah, her cousin, and the other shareholder had to elicit her help in recouping their losses. Drake and Jacob had done a very good job of warning off potential buyers.

Two months later, Hannah and her squad were indicted for subterfuge in buying and selling various companies around the country by fraudulent means. Every company ended up having just one share over and that share belonged to Hannah. Their accountant was also indicted for issuing false shares to gain control of the companies. She was found to be mentally incompetent and sentenced to a mental facility for the rest of her days. Her nephew never saw her again and after his time in prison, disappeared.

Cassie bought all shares from every shareholder and went private with GalUp, swearing to never offer to the public again. Six months after the buyout, GalUp was once again a raving success. With all the publicity over the past year, more people came to see what GalUp was all about. Cassie came back once a week to perform, even after the birth of her and Drake's three sets of twins.

They took Auntie's floor of the building and turned it into a learning center for women. It was designed to help them learn skills other than stripping or prostitution. Donors were abundant and they could not only house students on the remaining upper floors until transition, they were also able to pay the teachers as well.

Cassie ended her tenure at the university when the discovery of the second set of twins was announced. While her extracurricular activities had been proven not to affect her university duties, Cassie wanted to stay at home with her children. She was allowed to keep her research and contact with NASA, that turned out not to be very forthcoming with information other than she had her own star system. Tyler graduated and took over her classes, his dissertation proved she had taught well while at the university.

Drake and Cassie moved to her ranch, sold their in town homes, and invested in livestock. Wanting the best possible life for their kids, ranching seemed to be one of the options to try. They managed to purchase much of the original land back and named the ranch Gallup Farms. With more hands, they built new barns and bunkhouses for their expanding empire. Nothing like going all out for an endeavor neither knew anything about. But they both believed they were smart enough to learn. Cattle and thoroughbreds would make them wealthy and happy.

Many years after leaving GalUp, as Cassie sat viewing her ranch, a familiar voice spoke to her. It was soft, resonant, and comfortable. It was Mother Cassie.

"Hello, dear girl." The voice spoke, making Cassie smile. "I told you I would return when the time was right."

"You did." Cassie replied.

Mother Cassie laughed. "You've done amazing things with your life. I didn't remember six children. Three pregnancies, yes. The memory of an old woman."

"Oddly," Cassie shook her head, "three sets of twins. A good balance for each other."

"And for generations."

"True there. Is it my time?" Cassie questioned Mother Cassie.

"Oh, my stars no! It was just time for me to share and go."

"But we never chatted after that one time. Am I not to learn from you as well?"

"Dearling, the old saying, 'With age comes wisdom' has been fulfilled. You have learned so much and taught just as much, I think you are full to capacity." Mother Cassie's voice paused. "These new generations make me nervous. They need people like you to teach them."

"Oh." Cassie shook her head. "Those days are long past. I found my answers, sort of, and am content with my life."

"Bullshit!" Mother Cassie spit out. "You gaze longingly at the skies, wondering. I see it. Why don't you call them again?"

"I don't want to know."

"Call again. It's eating at you to know."

"NASA has better things to do than deal with an old astronomer."

"Girl," Mother Cassie's voice rose and became stern, "they called you this last time. This means they have something. Or at least questions about your star system."

Cassie watched her family and smiled. "I'm happy. Look at them all. This is my legacy to them and GalUp."

"Let me tell you," Mother Cassie sighed deeply, "you have a lot more years ahead of you. Full, productive, and exciting. Life has been very good to you. All your chapters have amazing endings except for one. The one you walked away from, never looking back. Now you're here with not much to do and wondering again. Wondering about parallel life or existence of other life. Period." Mother Cassie paused causing Cassie to wonder if she left. "I'm still here." Mother Cassie spoke.

"I thought you got mad and left." Cassie told her.

"I'm tougher than that." Mother Cassie snorted. "I may sound soft, but you seem to forget, we're made of sterner stuff than people want to believe."

Cassie chuckled.

"Before I go, listen carefully. Many things in the world have changed. You've seen this. Hell, you've been part of this little chapter of life, although you don't really know, just suspect. Life has changed. For everyone. You were the instigator. You found the reason for that change. When you walked away, the gap was not filled for years. But your daughter came along, and just like you, she found the stars. And her daughter is following. Together, they make a formidable team. You will be very proud of their discoveries."

"Your son has turned GalUp into one of the hottest entertainment venues and restaurants in this country. Not to mention the school he also runs. All of this is from your beginnings. You shared your dreams, and they ran with them. And look at your ranch. The others are doing amazing things just from your beginnings. Now you need to complete some of them yourself."

Cassie sat up higher. "How? Everything is in place, running smoothly without me. What can I do that will make things any better?"

"Darling," Cassie could feel a deep hug in that one word, "You will know when it's time to know. You'll feel it deep in your soul. You won't have to hunt or find a thing."

"I don't know where to start." Cassie moaned. "I just want peace and completion. I thought that's what I had."

"Well, peace you definitely have. Completion is coming. You just have to get off your old derriere and help it along a little. You're only 82, get up, get out, finish strong."

"Damn." Cassie shook her head. "Damn."

"You will be blessed beyond measure and learn some amazing things. I've said enough already so be prepared. Remember to look to the stars. Be safe dear self and enjoy the generations life is sharing with you. So much more will be coming to you soon."

Cassie felt Mother Cassie drift away. Gazing from her porch, she saw Drake on his way to her, smiling. She picked up her phone, found the number she was looking for, and placed a call. Part of her future smiled at her as she did so.

Don't miss out!

Visit the website below and you can sign up to receive emails whenever Katlyn Rose publishes a new book. There's no charge and no obligation.

https://books2read.com/r/B-A-TUJAB-AOBOC

BOOKS 2 READ

Connecting independent readers to independent writers.

Also by Katlyn Rose

Charlie's Children

Charlie's Children Neon Shadows 1

Charlie's Children: Guardian of the Lost 2

Charlie's Children: Age of Innocence 4

Charlie's Children: Shadows of the Past 3

Standalone

Starlight and Stilettos

Phoenix Rising: Thrive and Transform While in a Toxic Relationship

Chaos in the Kitchen

Moonbeam Chronicles: Witching Hour in Foxglove

When No One is Clapping for You, Clap for Yourself

About the Author

Raised in West Texas, Katlyn is a beacon of compassion, strength, and empowerment. With 35 years of marriage under her belt, Katlyn now resides on a small rural farm in Georgia, where she has dedicated her life to rescuing unloved animals, inspiring women, especially older women, to embrace their full potential, and expressing her creativity through the written word.

From a young age, Katlyn developed a deep connection with animals. Growing up in the Texas countryside, she witnessed the plight of abandoned and mistreated creatures, igniting a lifelong commitment to animal welfare. Now, on her small rural farm in Georgia, Katlyn has created a sanctuary where neglected animals find solace, healing, and a loving forever home.

Katlyn's passion for empowering older women stems from her belief that age should never be a barrier to personal growth and fulfillment. She loves guiding women on a transformative journey of self-discovery. Her support and encouragement inspire older women to embrace their unique strengths, unlock their hidden potential, and embark on new adventures with confidence and purpose.

In addition to her dedication to animal rescue and empowering older women, Katlyn finds solace and self-expression through writing. Her words flow effortlessly onto the page, capturing the essence of her experiences, insights, and the beauty she witnesses in the world around her. Through her writing, Katlyn aims to inspire others to embrace their passions, live authentically, and make a positive impact in their own lives and the lives of others.

Katlyn's life is her story of the power of compassion, strength, and the pursuit of one's passions. Through her undying commitment to rescuing unloved animals, empowering older women, and expressing her creativity through writing, she has become a guiding light for all who cross her path.

Her journey serves as an inspiration to embrace our true selves, live with purpose, and make a positive impact in the world, regardless of age or circumstance.